THE GOOD MAN

The Good Man

A heartwarming story of a young boy's journey to adulthood

PETER ALDERMAN

P & P Publishing

Copyright © 2022 by Peter Alderman

A special thanks to my patient editors: Patricia Alderman and
Kathryn Julian.

All rights reserved. No part of this book may be reproduced in any
manner whatsoever without written permission except in the case of
brief quotations embodied in critical articles and reviews.

This is a work of fiction. All of the characters,
organizations, and events portrayed in this novel
are either products of the author's imagination or used fictitiously.

First Printing, 2022

Printed in U.S.A.

Dedicated to our three sons, Chris, Shaun, and Jason who have grown up to be the epitome of The Good Man.

And to our seven grandsons, Brody, Branson, Quinn, Vaughn, River, Maxwell, and Xavior, whom we hope follow in their father's footsteps.

What readers are saying about *The Good Man:*

4.0 out of 5 stars. **A glimpse into what society could be today**
Peter describes heartfelt and somewhat old-fashioned ways to successfully negotiate the rigors of society. It's a warm and gracious story of 'give' rather than 'take'.

5.0 out of 5 stars **Always be considerate of others feelings**
The Good Man is a must read. When this young man (the protagonist) made a mistake, he admitted what he had done and learned from it. Strongly recommend *The Good Man*.

5.0 out of 5 stars **A Great Book**
A great book. Enjoy reading it.

5.0 out of 5 stars **Awesome!!**
A Great Book by a Great Author!!! Well Done.

5.0 out of 5 stars **A charming story from Peter Alderman**
I always enjoy the storytelling style of Peter Alderman. *The Good Man* is a charming coming of age tale and made for enjoyable easy reading. Nicely done.

5.0 out of 5 stars **Soothing**
The Good Man moves forward very smoothly. With each chapter, the reader is reminded of many situations he/she encountered during the early stages of life.

***The Good Man* is an especially important read right now** with our world being filled with so much strife and evil.

~ 1 ~

THE FUTURE

Prologue

It was a beautiful spring morning. The sun bathed the backyard with warmth, and its rays sliced through the window blinds creating a parallel pattern of light on the wooden kitchen floor. Carter sat at the table near the window with the same pattern of light resting on his face, his clothing.

He gazed out at the backyard and sighed. Their dog, Misty, lay on the warm, cement patio, oblivious to a rabbit hopping along the brook, stopping to munch on some greenery. A red cardinal fluttered down to the birdfeeder and helped himself to some seed. The tranquility of this moment reminded him of home. He loved nature, animals, and, especially, family.

He heard his wife in the kids' bedroom giggling and urging the boys to get ready for their naps. They began chuckling as she gently tickled with her finger tips. Then a muffled quiet engulfed the bedroom as the boys settled down. She switched on the white noise machine and tranquility subdued the little guys.

Carter smiled to himself. He got a kick out of those rascals. They were full of energy, mischief, and curiosity. And they smiled at everything and everybody.

But most of all, he loved his wife: her kindness, her gratefulness, her goodness. She was everything a man could ask for and more.

She shuffled quietly into the kitchen making sure she didn't wake the twins up. She looked at Carter with tenderness and gaze up at his wife, his beautiful, patient wife. He smiled and touched her hand as she sat down at the kitchen table and said, "It's been a journey, Honey. But look where we are."

She smiled back at Carter and laid her hand on his. "It has been a journey." She paused delicately, ". . . and you ended up with me."

"It was always you." He fidgeted, sighed, and gazed out the window, ". . . It was always you."

~ 2 ~

THE DIXON FARM - 1979

Paw Paw is a small town of about 3,300 people on the western side of Michigan. A drive from anywhere to the village of Paw Paw travels one past lush orchards and vineyards. The tranquility, open spaces, and calm embrace travelers as they near the center. Maple Lake fed by the Paw Paw River, sits in the heart of the community.

The village bustles with activities for visitors, from wine tasting to shopping in boutiques, to purchasing handmade crafts and even fresh baked goodies. Food options provide a variety of meals to appeal to anyone's taste buds.

The historic feel of the village is heartwarming, providing a vintage movie house, a local brewpub, and even a local community theater troupe.

The area's primary agricultural product is grapes used in the local wine industry and for juice and jellies. Farms, big and small, blanket the landscape. The Dixon farm was neither big nor small. It consisted of approximately twenty acres. Some land hugged the Paw Paw River, named by the Indians for the trees that once grew along its banks. The clearing of shade trees made the Paw Paw trees less common. The attempted planting of the trees at the high school failed because of the school's abundance of sun's rays and the needed soil conditions to grow the Paw Paw. In topographical history, the effort to reach back slipped away in a noble attempt.

The Dixon Farm was one of those farms in Paw Paw. The family grew some grapes but primarily raised livestock such as cattle, pigs, and goats. Emmitt Dixon had inherited the farm in 1979 at only eighteen years old. His father married late and was aging and needed his only son to take over the business.

Emmitt was a quiet, thoughtful man, a man of few words. However, when he was young, he was energetic and in love in high school. Rachel, a pretty student, was in the same English class he or is it him. She was sweet, petite, and kind. Her blonde hair stretched to her shoulders, and her smile lit up the room. Emmitt was beyond himself with love. He was not going to let Rachel slip away.

After high school, they got married in a small wedding at the farm with family and a few chickens wandering around. His father wore his 'clean overalls' for the occasion. He was a quirky guy, and his overalls were his identity. The simplicity of the celebration was perfect. It was more than enough for them. They were happy and in love.

Rachel had attended Bronson School of Nursing in Kalamazoo. She was able to get her associates degree in nursing and worked briefly at Bronson Lake View Hospital in Paw Paw. The following year they had a bouncing baby boy and named him Carter. Two years later, Carter was joined by a baby brother whom they named Damon.

It was a busy, hectic life raising two children and working the farm, but they were happy and Emmitt's dad, better known as Grampy at this point, loved the boy.

~ 3 ~

CHANGE

That happiness melted away quickly after two tragic events. First, Emmitt's father passed away from a heart attack when trying to corral some of the cattle. The first responders, police, EMTs, tried valiantly to save him but to no avail.

That was heartbreaking. Rachel was never sure if Emmitt would get over the loss of his dad. His father was the only family he had since his mother died giving birth to him.

That was followed by one of the most horrific events in America's history: the attack on the Twin Towers and the Pentagon on September 11, 2011. JoDee Messina's song "Heaven Must Be Needing a Hero" played relentlessly on the radio. The message was like a drumbeat in Emmitt's head. He was consumed with anger. Sadness over losing his father wrapped Emmitt's mind. Guilt throbbed in his heart for not being there for his father when he died. Emmitt needed something to fill that void and to do something about the attack on the Twin Towers.

Emmitt loved America and all it stood for: freedom, opportunity, equality. However, he felt an obligation to protect his country, and he also needed something to steer his mind away from his father's death. So, he enlisted into the army, and that was that.

In a way, it was selfish. He had two children and a wife. Rachel's parents helped out, but it was difficult. Nonetheless, he did it.

Emmitt ended up in Northern Iraq, fighting with the Kurds against Isis. Northern Iraq extends north from Baghdad, bordered by Syria, Turkey, and Iran.

The Kurds have been attacked, displaced, and discriminated against throughout the years, yet they have survived. As Carter found out, they are fierce fighters, loving people, and welcoming to others.

Two Kurdish soldiers, in particular, Hemen and Mizgeen, became very close to Emmitt when he was ripped apart by shrapnel from a roadside bomb near the city of Arbil. They had carried him away out of harm's way and cared for his wounds. Then, they brought him back to their village of Zaktu, which was further north and deeper into Kurdish land. When Emmitt got there, the Kurdish people treated him like royalty. Hemen's and Mizgeen's cousins, Diyan, Nawaf, and Shakir, would come into the home with food and support. Smiles, laughter, and a sense of family embraced him. Daresh, a pretty Kurdish girl with dark, flowing hair, was extremely comforting and intrigued Emmitt with her flirtatious eyes. She was good as a caretaker. She was even better at being a fierce soldier. Kurdish women fought alongside their brothers as equals.

Here he was in a strange land, surrounded by people of different ethnicity, foreign language, traditions. They were Sunni Muslims, yet he felt a sense of family. He missed home. He missed *his* family.

Emmitt was discharged honorably from the army because of his injuries. Rick Rex, his high school buddy, picked him up at the Kalamazoo airport and drove him to the farm. Emmitt gazed out the truck's window. The sight of cornfields, horses, cows, farms filled his heart. His senses came alive. He never was going to leave this place again. But, man! He was glad to be back home.

When they got to the Dixon ranch, Rachel and the boys were seated on the back porch. Rachel was more beautiful than he had even remembered. Carter and Damon nestled beside her. Emmitt got out of the truck, and before he could even shut the door, they had run up to Emmitt, flocked around him, and hugged. Rachel had tears running down her cheeks. But she wasn't the only one. Emmitt did as well as he wiped his eyes with his sleeve.

"I will never leave you, Rachel. I am so sorry."

"I know. You did what you had to do at the time to escape your pain."

"It was selfish of me." He looked down at the boys. Carter looked up at him, smiled, and hugged his leg. Damon remained a little distant. He wasn't even sure who this man was. ". . . and I will always be there for you two guys." He knelt, hugged them, and kissed them both on their cheeks. When he stood up, he held Rachel tightly in his arms. "I will never leave you, Rachel."

Nine months later, the Dixon's welcomed a little girl, Emily, into their lives.

~ 4 ~

FARM CHORES

Emmitt adopted his father's tradition of wearing overalls in honor of his dad. He wore them all the time: one for work and a clean pair for special occasions. However, his attire did not make work on the farm any easier.

Emmitt desperately tried to keep it as a working farm, but farming was not an easy life and the seasons were not always kind. But their two sons, Carter, Damon, and their daughter, Emily, although young, and his sweet wife, Rachel, worked all hours to keep the livestock fed, the grapes growing, and the repairs to the equipment and buildings addressed.

It had rained the night before, leaving the ground wet and muddy. These were perfect conditions for Carter and his brother to partake in one of their favorite games: chasing the pigs.

The screeching of the boys and the pigs vibrated through the house. Their father, Emmitt, just shook his head as he stared out the kitchen window at the muddy chaos by the barn. "Looks like they're at it again, Rachel."

She smiled and held Emmitt's hand. "Yes! They are something else." Rachel was used to it. She had seen this event play over and over again throughout the years. She was just grateful that their daughter, Emily, wasn't into that sort of thing. She was all girl. Although she liked the animals and helped with the chores around the farm, she preferred reading, playing video games, and doing girl things. "They're having the time of their life. Oh. It looks like they may have company."

Riding up to the barn was a young, gangly girl. She was on top of a horse much too big for her. Her long, black hair bounced up and down as the horse trotted toward the barn. The boys shouted out gleefully from their mud paradise when they spotted her. "Hey, Charli! Come join us."

Charli was the girl who lived on the farm down the road. She was spunky and a year younger than Carter. She helped her parents on the farm and watched her little brother, Eric, who had down syndrome. She was a combination of toughness and compassion.

Charli hopped off her horse with a big grin and tied him to the fence. "I'm not going to get these nice jeans dirty," she grinned sheepishly. She then opened the door to the pen, dashed up to the boys, and dove into the mud.

"You're crazy, Charli," said Carter.

"Not as crazy as you two loons."

"Watch this!!" Carter took off after one of the pigs, who quickly turned to the left. Carter dug in his heels and adjusted, but the pig suddenly lurched to the side. So again, Carter cut in that direction, leaped into the air, and tackled the pig. Carter looked up and grinned from his muddy position, the squealing pig wrapped in his hands, "How's that?"

Charli looked at Damon with mud dripping down her face, "Your brother is crazy."

Damon replied, "Actually, Charli, I think we're all a little ditzy."

~ 5 ~

HALLOWEEN

It was fall, and one of the most important events of the year was about to take place: Halloween. Eric was over the top with excitement. He loved Spiderman and got a new costume for trick-or-treating. The entire gang was going out as superheroes. Charli was going as Bat Woman, Carter as Batman, Damon as the Hulk, and Emily as, well, . . . a princess.

They all met at Charli's house. Charli's mom cooked popcorn for all of the guests. Spiderman was chasing Batman. The Hulk and Bat Woman were munching on the goodies, and the princess was touching up her hair.

Mr. Rex came out with his phone and requested that all the guests surround the dining room table decorated with ghosts, witches, and the fall leaves. "OK, Superheroes, get ready with a big smile." Then he hesitated, "Hey, Mrs. Rex."

"Honey, you can call me Hope," she smiled.

"OK, Hope. You hop in there as well, next to the princess. It is always good to have two princesses in a picture." He grinned, pleased with his humor.

Charli's parents, Rick and Hope Rex, were good-natured people. They were also kind people willing to help others whenever needed. The Dixons and the Rexes got together for cookouts whenever possible, but farming made those events limited. The harsh, cold winters of Michigan didn't help with socializing either.

When Carter had gone off to war, the Rex family helped Rachel care for the boys. A family bond developed between the children and the families. It was a feeling of security that there was help beyond the fences, the pastures that one could count on for support.

Mr. Rex drove the kids to town to do their trick-or-treating. All the kids sat in the pickup bed, which had a layer of hay to cushion their ride. As they passed other 'ghosts and goblins," shrieks and laughs rose from the riders.

Trick-or-treating was great. Paw Paw stores opened their doors for the kids walking the streets and handed out goodies.

Eric leaned on Carter's arm while they both munched on candy on the way home. "How are you doing, Buddy?" Carter said to his little friend. Eric looked up with happy eyes, "Good. Real good." The other trick-or-treaters, Charli, Damon, and Emily, compared candy hauls as the moon lit up the sky and stars glanced down to guide their way. It was a Norman Rockwell image and a night to remember. Family, friends, and memories. The good ole days.

~ 6 ~

FRIDAY NIGHT LIGHTS

Two years slip by quickly, quietly when you're young. Charli was now fourteen, as was Damon.

Carter had just turned fifteen and enjoyed his first year in high school, even though he struggled in some classes. He had been diagnosed with ADHD, Attention-Deficit/Hyperactive Disorder, when Carter was in sixth grade. He had needed help throughout his school years. But Carter was passing.

He had joined the football team and proved to be quite a capable receiver. The lanky teen lacked blistering speed, but Carter could catch anything thrown his way. Also, he could always find the open field. Once the ball was in his hands, he would cut, pivot, and leap for extra yardage.

It seemed as though the entire town of 3,000 would turn out for Friday night games at the Paw Paw High School's Falan Stadium, named after a legendary former coach. The Dixon family sat in the stands with all the other fans to cheer on their Red Wolves, especially number 85. Yes! Carter Dixon: their favorite player. Number 85 was Greg Jenning's number when he played for the Packers. Carter had watched him perform professionally and saw his poster in the Football Hall of Fame at Western Michigan. He said to himself when he was younger *I'm going to wear that number: 85*

He felt a little guilty not wanting to wear Paw Paw's and former Western Michigan player Jason Babin's number. He was a former NFL Pro-bowl player, a linebacker: big, strong, and powerful. Carter was none of those.

In this game, Carter had been the target of 6 passes, and he hauled them all in for 105 yards and one touchdown. Paw Paw won the game 24 to 21 on a last-minute field goal. The pack stormed the field, and a sea of fans swallowed up the players. Emmitt and Rachel quietly sat in the stands watching the commotion below them. Damon, Emily, and Charli, who grabbed her little brother's hand, had joined the mess slapping Carter on his shoulder pads as he smiled, holding his helmet. Finally, Eric peeked up from the group. Carter smiled down at him and patted him on the head.

Emmitt and Rachel rested on their sofa at home, waiting for Carter and the clan to return. Emmitt had errands to do in the morning and needed some rest but he wanted to say good night to his kids. Suddenly, the kitchen door popped open, and their children were still celebrating the win.

Once they settled down a bit, mom said, "OK, kids. Time to hit the sack. It's getting late."

"OK, mom," and they headed for their rooms. Carter was trailing his siblings and slapping them fives as they turned to face him.

"Hey, Carter!" Can I talk with you?"

"Sure, Dad." He turned, walked up to the sofa, and took a seat by his father. "What's up?"

"I'm proud of you."

"Thanks, Dad."

"You played another great game," he paused. "You had a lot of people cheering you on."

"Yah! That was cool."

"But, Carter." He leaned closer to his son.

Sensing something odd, Carter focused on his father. "Yes, Sir?"

"You're not a big deal."

"Sir?" His father had just taken the air out of his tires. Carter wasn't upset but curious about what his dad had on his mind. His father was not a malicious person. He was steady, measured, and instructive. Carter listened intently.

"You did great, and we're proud of you. But don't get a big head. I'm not saying that you are, but keep it level. Maintain your composure and be modest."

Carter grinned at his father, "Yes, Dad."

"You are fortunate that you have the abilities that you have. You worked hard, but achieving anything takes talent and hard work." Carter nodded his head in agreement. Then, his father pressed on, "There are kids in your school who play in the band to support the team. Some cheerleaders root you all on. Some teachers help you with your studies. Some coaches make you a better player. And . . .," a slight pause, "there are kids who can't do half the things you can for one reason or another but have something special to offer. Am I clear, Carter?" he said with a gentle smile.

Carter's mind immediately drifted to Charli's little brother, Eric, who had down syndrome. Carter knew full well that he was fortunate to be able to do all the things that he could do. He looked at his dad and responded respectfully, "Yes, Dad," then stood up and grinned, "but maybe a little bit of a big deal."

"OK. A little bit of a big deal. But always value those you come in contact with, for they too are a 'big deal' in their way. Now, get out of here." He chuckled as he threw a cushion at his son. Carter was headed toward his bedroom when his father said, "Carter, . . . you're a big deal to us."

"Thanks, Dad," Carter grinned. "Good night."

"Good night, son."

Rachel came up behind Emmitt as he sat on the couch. She massaged his shoulders. "You're a good father, Emmitt, . . . and a big deal." He smiled and patted her hand.

"Was that too much?"

"I don't think so. I believe Carter got the message: Humility."

~ 7 ~

RAIN, RAIN GO AWAY

The boys and their father rode the horses out to the pasture. The cows were roaming everywhere in the fields. They had to herd the cattle and get them all back into the barn. The forecast that evening was for driving rain and heavy wind—no time for livestock or humans to be outside. Charli had ridden her horse, Midnight, over to the Dixon home earlier and was also trying to help. They rustled all the cattle to the barn. However, some of the goats had wandered off, spooked by the blasts of thunder.

It was starting to sprinkle. Then a heavy rain pelted the ground. The footing was sloppy, and the horses struggled to keep their balance. Emmitt yelled through the storm for everyone to get back to the barn except for Carter. His horse, Whisper, was the most reliable and steady out of all of them.

Emmitt had trouble controlling his horse. The thunderclaps were just too much for his steed. Finally, he yelled to Carter, "I have to take this ole mule back. He's too skittish."

"'I'm good, dad. I'll see you at the house."

After a while, the rain intensified with a downpour that made it nearly impossible to see. A flash of lightning followed by a blast of thunder startled Whisper. She reared up on her hind legs, practically throwing Carter from his saddle. He managed to hang on and settled her, and continued his search for the goat. Eventually, he could hear squealing in the darkness. He followed the urgent whine that pierced through the storm. He knew he had to act quickly.

Damon and Charli raced their horses to the barn. They hopped off their animals, and Damon began to take off his horse's saddle. Emmitt then trotted into the barn, leaning over to calm his horse down patting his mane.

"Where's Carter?" Charli yelled.

"He'll be back. He's just getting. . ."

Charli then jumped back onto her horse.

"What are you doing?" yelled Damon.

"I'm not going to let Carter be out there alone."

"Don't go, Charli" Emmitt screamed.

It was too late. Charli and her horse had thundered out of the barn, not listening to Mr. Dixon nor knowing where she was heading.

Meanwhile, Carter had followed the cries of the goat. Whisper was steady and reliable. She trotted in the direction Carter guided her. The rushing currents of the Paw Paw River filled the air, accompanied by the wails of animals in horror.

Suddenly, Carter saw two goats. One was at the edge of the water. Her eyes bulged with fear. She was staring at her partner. That goat was clinging to the side of the river bank with rising water rushing over her back. Carter leaped off of Whisper and slushed through the mud toward the goat. He held onto the Whisper's reins as he reached out to grab the goat's horns.

Behind him, he could hear hooves splashing coming toward him.

"Carter, I'm here," yelled Charli. She slid off of her horse and ran toward him. Carter just focused on the goat, wondering how he would save him.

Carter's father pulled up just about the same time. He had a rope with him and threw it to Carter to lope around the goat's neck. Carter took the rope and put it around the goat's neck. He then leaped up onto Whisper, secured the rope to his saddle, and pulled the goat as Emmitt and Charli guided him out of the water. The rain mitigated to a steady drizzle at this point.

When the goat was safe and secure on the land, Carter slid off Whisper. Charli ran up and draped her arms around him. "Are you OK, Carter?"

"I'm fine, Charli," he said with a smile. "Don't get weird on me now."

Emmitt just watched as he hoisted himself onto his horse, tying the other goat up.

~ 8 ~

TALK WITH DAD

The trio wiped the horses in the barn and settled them into the stables. Damon had gone into the house to update his mom about what was happening.

Carter looked at Charli, "Charli, you should have stayed in the barn."

"I know, but I couldn't help myself. I was..."

"I appreciate that, but if you ever got hurt out there," he looked out the barn door as rain poured down, "I would never have forgiven myself."

"I agree with Carter," Emmitt interjected. "I told you to stay in the barn."

"... but I ..."

"Just listen, Charli. We care about you and don't want you to get hurt."

Carter watched as Charli responded, "I'm sorry, Mr. Dixon." Her head dropped down, looking at the straw on the barn floor.

"Let's go inside and get dried off. Then, we'll let your parents know how you are," said Emmitt.

When everyone got back into the home, they toweled off as much as possible. Rachel had prepared a spaghetti dinner for everyone, but they were all too wet to sit down then, and Charli had to get home. She was dripping wet. Charli texted her parents and let them know that Carter and Mr. Dixon would drive her to her house since it was still raining. Midnight would have a sleepover in the barn with the other horses. Charli would have to stay over another time for dinner when they weren't all drenched.

Mr. Dixon, Carter, and Charli squeezed into the front seat of the old Ford truck sitting just outside the barn. It was still drizzling with specks of sun trying to peek out from the parting clouds. A mist started to rise from the fields in the distance. It was a scene of serenity in contrast to the storm that had hammered down on them earlier.

"Thanks for helping, Charli," said Mr. Dixon.

Sheepishly, Charli responded, "Thank you for caring. It was a little wonky out there for the horses in the mud. I'm glad we all made it back."

"Me, too," inserted Carter. "I have to admit that I was pretty nervous trying to get those goats out of the river. The rushing water seemed to keep on rising."

"We were all lucky," said Emmitt. "Sometimes that river can be unpredictable and scoop a person away instantly. Next time, we've got to make sure that all animals are counted."

"Sorry, Dad. I should have taken care of them before the storm."

His father grinned as he looked over at him, "We all make mistakes, and this won't be your last." He turned the truck onto the long, muddy driveway leading to Charli's house. "We're here, Charli. Say hello to your parents and Eric for us."

"Sure will, Mr. Dixon. She glanced at Carter, "Bye, Carter."

Carter smiled and nodded his head. He and his father watched the thin teenager hop the steps onto her front porch. She turned and waved with a grinning face. The strands of her hair were still wet and matted against her cheeks. Charli's mom, Mrs. Rex, opened the door. Behind her, Eric peeked out at the truck. The three of them waved goodbye as the old Ford splashed through the puddles in the driveway.

The two of them drove for a while without talking, just reviewing the day's events in their heads. Finally, after some time, Emmitt broke the silence, "She's a nice girl," as he glanced at Carter.

Carter stared straight ahead with a big grin, "Sure is. She's a great buddy."

"She's cute, too."

"Yeah. I guess."

Emmitt responded, "Is she more than a 'buddy', Carter?"

"Nooo, Dad. Charli is my best friend."

"Do you love her?"

"Yikes, Dad. Where are you going with this?" His face started to turn red.

Emmitt looked at Carter. I just want you to be good to her."

"Dad, I will," he blurted with surprise. "She is my buddy, and I love her like . . . "he paused as they pulled into their yard by the barn. It was dark now, and little sister Emily stood out on the back porch under the light, waving welcoming them home.

Emmitt finished Carter's sentence for him, ". . . like a sister."

Carter pondered his dad's statement, "That's right. . . . Like a sister." Then, he smiled in the direction of Emily.

His dad then said, "Good. Treat all women with love and respect as you would for your sister."

He looked back at his dad. "I gotcha," he smiled and poked him in the shoulder with his fist. "Like my sister." He slid out of the truck and ran up to give 'his sister' a hug.

~ 9 ~

JUNIOR YEAR SUMMER

A cool breeze drifted off of Lake Michigan. The air was fresh and clean. The corn growing across the river swayed. The stalks appeared choreographed in dance to the rhythm of the wind. Carter and Charli sat by the river's edge with fishing poles stretched out over the water. Behind them, their horses, Midnight and Whisper, hung their heads, chewing on grass.

"Do you think we'll catch anything, Carter?"

"Could be. The water is flowing gently, and there are some logs over there." He pointed, "Fish like to hang around those branches. By the way, Charli. It doesn't matter if we catch anything or not. It's a beautiful day."

"You're right."

They both looked over the water watching their lines as ripples meandered around the stretches of nylon. The sun peeked through the Paw Paw trees and reflected off of the water. It was peaceful. It was comfortable. It was midwest magic that both Carter and Charli sensed as something special.

Still looking out at his line, Carter asked, "How's Eric doing?" Charli was silent, staring out over the water. Carter tried again, "Charli, how's Eric?"

Charli looked up at Carter. Water was pooling in her eyes. "He's OK."

"What does that mean?" Charli said nothing and sucked in a deep breath of air. "Come on, Charli. Let me know so I can help if I can."

"It's nothing, Carter. Let's just fish."

"Charli, you are my best friend. I'm not going to 'just fish' when you are hurtin' inside. Please tell me what's going on."

Charli looked up at Carter. Her eyes were bloodshot from the tears that now streamed down her face. Carter extended his arm around her and patted her shoulder gently.

"Thank you, Carter. You're right."

"I'm here for you, Charli. Just start talking as long as you're comfortable doing so."

She took in another deep breath and said, "Well, you know how Eric had his bagging job at the grocery store."

"Yeah."

"Well, he got in trouble," Charli choked.

"Trouble! Eric wouldn't do anything wrong. What happened?"

"A mother came through the register line with her little boy in the shopping cart," Charli paused, ". . . and Eric smiled at him and patted the little boy on his head softly."

"And . . . ?"

". . . and the mother erupted and snapped at Eric, "Don't touch my baby."

"Then what?"

"Eric jumped back in shock. He was confused and hurt at the same time."

". . . What happened next?"

"Eric was suspended for two weeks. He still doesn't know what happened or what he did wrong."

"He didn't do anything wrong, Charli. I'll talk to Eric and get him back on track."

"It was just so mean. How could anybody be so mean to an innocent down syndrome boy who gives nothing but love to others?"

"My mother was saying that some people are hurting inside. Then, they transfer that hurt to others. Mom told me to try to treat everybody with kindness. If they continue to be mean, you have to continue to be kind to, hopefully, chip away at their hurt."

"Sounds pretty deep to me," Charli sighed. And pretty dumb in this case, she thought to herself.

"It's not. Everybody carries some burden. My mother said that we should never add to someone's hurting. Instead, people should try to empathize and understand others."

"Well, I don't understand, Carter."

"Nor do I. Nor do I have to. I just want to be the one who does the right thing, to help possibly."

"Oh, Carter. Why can't you just get pissed off like a normal person? Maybe you will after you hear this." He lifted his head with heightened interest. "The woman pushed her cart up with her little boy to customer service. She blasted, 'That boy,' pointing to Eric, sitting Indian style on the floor, rocking back and forth with his face cupped over his teary eyes, 'that boy,' she repeated, 'abused my son and should be fired.' She paused momentarily, stared at the customer service manager, and blasted, 'Why do you hire freaks like that anyway?' She then turned and stormed out the door with her groceries and kid.

So, Carter, who do you think is hurting?" she nearly screamed.

Carter's face became red with anger. Something Charli had never seen before. He gritted his teeth and hissed, "That woman is not hurt. That woman is F'N crazy."

"Holy cow, Carter. I've never heard you swear before."

"I didn't swear."

"Yes, you did."

"I said, F'N'. That's not a swear."

"You know what you meant."

"I didn't swear."

"Oh, Carter. You bad boy."

"Knock it off, Charli."

Just then, Charli's line tightened. Then, her pole began to bend.

"Pull it, Charli." She tugged, and the fish swam wildly around. Then, as she began to reel it into shore, the fish twisted loose, and the line went limp. "Oh, Charli."

"Win a few. Lose a few," Charli chirped. She was just as happy. She hated taking the fish off of the hook. Then, after a few minutes, Charli asked, "Carter, what are you going to do after you graduate this year?"

"I'm not sure. Dad wants me to go off to college. He wants me to get as many skills as I can. He's afraid that farming doesn't provide a lot of options, and it will be too tough of a life."

"Yikes. Your dad sounds like my dad. He's having a rough time making ends meet with the unpredictable seasons."

"But you know, Charli. I like this life. It is hard sometimes and unpredictable, but look around." His hand stroked the air like a conductor at the gently flowing river, the waving corn, and the blue sky. "I would miss this big time if I didn't farm."

"Me, too."

They were both lost in thought, looking out at their lines dangling in the water. One of the horses snorted behind them. They both were startled. Their thoughts dispersed, and they started laughing.

Carter looked over at his best friend, "Charli, we're moving onto another phase of our lives."

"Yes, we are," she smiled. "But wherever you go, I'll always be your best friend."

"Same here," Carter softly said. ". . . Same here. And Charli."

"Yes?"

"I'll talk to my buddy, Eric."

Charli smiled and gave Carter a hug.

"Don't get weird on me, Charli."

~ 10 ~

THE 2016 PRESIDENTIAL DEBATES

The talk around the town and, for that matter, the talk around the state was all about the presidential election and the candidates, Hillary Clinton and Donald Trump. However, this conversation got little traction in the Dixon household. Emmitt and Rachel have always been very private about their political views and leaned more on what was happening on the farm and with family.

When the kids had come home from school, they opened a political can of worms by asking about which candidate would be best for president. Both Emmitt and Rachel had shied away from such interactions. However, the topic had come up in school as part of their civics lesson. Every four years, the kids vote at school for the candidate they think would make the president. The vote would be confidential, but the kids took this assignment seriously.

When they got home from school, the three siblings poured into the kitchen and were bantering around their preferred candidate.

"I would vote for Hillary," said Emily.

"Are you kidding me!" blurted Damon. "Do you think that she is really qualified?"

"Yes. I do." Emily squared her shoulders and stretched her body a little taller. "Hillary was the Secretary of State and had to deal with many important people."

"Well, Trump has great business experience and built his real estate company up from nothing," pushed Damon.

Carter kept quiet, taking in the talking points and observing his younger sister and brother debate their perceived qualifications of the candidates. Emmitt leaned against the kitchen sink counter, and Rachel stood next to him.

Damon then asked Carter, "What do you think, Carter?"

"Yeah, Carter. What do you think?" quipped Emily.

The kitchen became quiet. Emmitt and Rachel were interested in Carter's response. So were Damon and Emily. All eyes were on him. Carter felt pressure but said in a relaxed response, "I need to know more about each of them."

The family had ended up in the living room. Rachel had begun working at Bronson Lake View Hospital. However, she was home this evening. Everyone was gathered around the TV watching the debate between Ms. Clinton and Mr. Trump. Megyn Kelly from FOX news was hosting the event. Her opening question was a dilly and directed to Donald Trump. She asked, "Is calling women 'fat pigs, dogs, slobs, and disgusting animals' behavior befitting a president?"

The questions sparked a furious reaction from Trump, who responded by attempting to camouflage his anger by injecting humor, saying that he only called Rosie O'Donnell those names.

The siblings all looked at each other with curious faces.

Emily scowled, "Did he really call women those names?" The question was launched into the air to nobody in particular.

Emmitt calmly got up from the sofa, walked over to the TV, and shut it off. "It's getting late."

"But we have to vote. How are we going to know who to vote for?" Damon shrugged.

Before the election, there will be plenty of opportunities to watch more debates and research the candidates.

Carter could tell his father had absorbed a reaction to the debate but wasn't sure how he felt. "Dad, are you a Republican or a Democrat?"

"Neither," he smiled. Rachel watched the conversation curiously.

"How can that be?" asked Emily.

"Well, I'm independent."

"What's that?" pursued Emily.

"An Independent doesn't vote for the party. Instead, they vote for whom they think is the best candidate."

Damon spoke, "How can you tell who the best candidate is?"

Emmitt paused and selected his words carefully, "When you vote, you look for the person who is respectful with others and poised in difficult situations. But most of all, you vote for someone who has the most integrity."

"What's integrity?" asked Emily.

"Integrity is the quality of being honest and having strong moral principles. Simply put, it is a person who is understanding, fair, and does the right thing whether someone is watching or not." Emmitt looked at his children and then his wife. "Like your mom." She smiled back at him. "And like I want all of you to be every day, every hour, and every minute."

Rachel stood up and shooed their children in the direction of their rooms, "Now, get to bed." They shuffled off, talking amongst each other, still consumed with questions.

Rachel looked up at her husband and gave him a hug.

~ 11 ~

SENIOR FOOTBALL SEASON AT PAW PAW

The football season had gone well. Carter had scored 14 touchdowns and had caught a total of 54 passes. He was recognized as a First Team All-Conference player and even got a spot on the Second Team All-Region roster. Carter had received interest from several Division 2 schools. However, he wanted to stay close to home and hoped that he would play at WMU. It was nearby and was in Division I. Carter wanted to challenge himself to see if he could play at that level.

"Dad, what should I do? I want to play Division I but haven't heard from any schools at that level."

"Son, you have heard from a bunch of excellent schools. Grand Rapids has a great team, and Michigan Tech, Wayne State, and Hilldale College are good schools."

"But, I really ... "

Emmitt cut him off, "Carter; you will end up where you belong. Be grateful you have so many choices."

"You're right, dad."

"Now quit whining and do something productive," his father smiled as he pointed to the barn and beyond.

Carter's dream of playing division one football did not end at the kitchen table. However, there was someone behind the scenes trying to help his former player out.

Carter's high school coach, Dennis Strey, cared for his players during the game and beyond the field. He was encouraging and supportive. In confidence, the coach had contacted Coach Lester of WMU and told him about Carter's interest in playing for him. Coach Lester was receptive to the idea, especially after viewing some football highlights of Carter's senior year. He had been on WMU's radar all along but not enough to be offered an outright scholarship. However, his skills were impressive enough to get him on the turf at Waldo Stadium as a preferred walk-on.

Carter was out in the barn mucking up the stalls. He didn't mind that smelly chore. He was just grateful they had horses. It was worth the stench.

His father was calling his name from the back porch. "Carter, you have a phone call."

"Who is it?" He thought it might be Charli.

Emmitt held the phone out in his hand like a dog biscuit as Carter came running toward him. "You'll find out."

On the line a voice asked, "Hello. Is this Carter Dixon?"

"Yes. It is," Carter responded.

"Hi, Carter, I'm Coach Lester from Western Michigan."

Carter almost dropped the phone. "Yes, Sir?"

"We've watched some film of your games. Very impressive."

"Thank you, Sir," Carter grinned at his father and pointed to the phone with his free hand.

"Well, we would like to know if you would accept a preferred walk-on offer to be a part of the Bronco family." Emmitt smiled at his son as he watched him glow with excitement.

"Oh, my goodness, coach. I wanted that so much. Yes! Thank you, and yes."

"We'll make arrangements for you to meet with us and get everything squared away."

"Thank you, Coach. Thank you so much."

"Welcome to WMU, Carter."

Carter hung up the phone and ran up to his father, picked him up, and swung him around.

'Save those tackles for the field," chuckled Emmitt.

~ 12 ~

BEING THANKFUL

    The football season was over. It was time for Carter to focus on school and farm chores. It was Sunday. It was his turn to feed the pigs. Clouds swallowed up the sun. Carter looked up at the sky. Dark cumulus clouds were forming and occupying most of what was once blue. There was a crisp wind. It was getting colder. Emily was helping him, and he asked her, "Is it going to storm tonight?"
    Emily was always on her computer looking up things, and the weather report was one of those things. "I believe so, Carter. We're supposed to get snow."
    "How much?"
    "It could be as much as ten inches," Emily smiled, "or as little as five."
    "Wow. That means we might not have school," Carter grinned.
    ". . . And we might have school," Emily retorted. She liked school. Emily wanted to learn, study, and be aware of what was happening and what had happened in the past. Carter, not so much. He was content with just getting by, which did not please his parents.

"I heard that two things determine if we have school or not," said Carter.

"And what are those?" Emily asked curiously.

"Well, one is if there are more than ten inches of snow, and, . . ." he grinned sheepishly.

"And what?"

". . . and, I should say, or if the superintendent can't open his door to get out because the snow is piled up too high.

"Interesting!" Emily responded.

"Very." Carter's grin widened.

The snow fell delicately at just about noontime. Emmitt was seated on the sofa in the living room, staring at the TV, hoping to catch an update on the weather. Rachel came out of the kitchen holding a mug.

"Here's some coffee, Emmitt."

"Thank you."

"Have you heard any mention about the storm and how much we might get?"

"Yes! It looks like the boys will have to go out shoveling Mrs. Barbieri's walkway late in the night when the snow has accumulated. Mrs. Barbieri was the sweet, older woman who lived alone a mile down the road and was affectionately called Dottie B by the Dixons and everyone in town. She was a fixture in the community, and everyone knew her. She would attend sporting events, bake cookies for the police and fire department, bring flowers to those who were sick. She was the best.

She never wanted to leave her cottage. It was home. Everyday memories of her late husband, her children, and the few animals they had danced in her mind to give her joy. It was a small plot of land. It was *her* plot of paradise.

Emmitt and the family checked in on her from time to time, brought her vegetables, helped with small chores, talked to her about her two children who lived in other states. A son and a daughter.

Her son lived in Franklin, Tennessee. He was in real estate and had done exceptionally well as the market had skyrocketed in recent years. He had some fancy clients, too, like Jason Aldean and Blake Shelton, famous country singers, and Keith Urban and Nicole Kidman, who had lived out in Leiper's Fork in Franklin.

Her daughter was married with three children and lived in California. Dottie B. had pictures of her grandchildren throughout different stages of their lives on tables, the fireplace mantel, and on the walls. Her family was everything to her, and she was everything to her family. Her son provided for her financially, and her daughter often called as did her grandchildren. However, she was alone, and the Dixon family filled in the gaps to make her life more comfortable, more secure.

Mr. Dixon had just pulled in the driveway from doing some errands. Mrs. Dixon had prepared a typical Sunday meal for them: roast beef, potatoes, green beans, and an apple pie for dessert.

They were blessed. Every night they had a tradition of holding hands while seated at the dining room table, and each family member offered thanks for what they had in their lives. They usually started with the youngest, Emily, but they would begin if anyone were especially eager to share their thanks about something. Tonight, Carter jump-started the tradition, "I'm really thankful it is snowing," he grinned.

"Well. That's nice," said Rachel. "Is there anything else you'd like to add?"

"Sure! And I'm thankful for this wonderful dinner that mom made for everyone."

The other members spoke in turn, highlighting what they were grateful for. Emily was happy that taking care of the pigs was done. Damon was glad that he had finished his homework. Rachel was thrilled to be with her children and her husband, and Emmitt was happy to have a warm house surrounded by family on this cold winter night.

~ 13 ~

SNOWSTORM

Shoveling snow for a path for Dottie B. usually occurred around 3:00 in the morning. By then, there had been enough snow amassed to require shoveling. The snow had accumulated to the point that driving would be difficult, if not downright dangerous. Damon didn't want to go, so Carter called Charli if she would like to help after dinner. He knew the answer even before talking with her. She was always up for something different.

Emmitt suggested that they take horses and strap the aluminum shovels to their backs like a bow.

The alarm went off at 2:30 in the morning in Carter's room, nearly waking Damon. Damon rolled around, groaned, and went back to sleep. Carter got up, dressed warmly with insulated pants, work boots, and a heavy jacket. Before leaving the house, he grabbed his cowboy hat and headed out to the barn to get Whisper. He was ready.

The snow had accumulated to roughly eight inches. Good call by dad to take the horses. It was lightly coming down like feathers falling from the sky. It was cold but not freezing, and the wind had subsided to a whimper.

Carter rode his horse out of the barn into the weather. Whisper seemed to enjoy trotting in the snow. The plows had already been busy pushing snow to the sides of the roads. On the way to Charli's house, Carter dug out three fire hydrants covered with piling, white mounds.

When he got to Charli's house, she was already waiting to go with Midnight saddled and wanting to get out. Looking at his hat, she kidded, "Hi, Cowboy. What took you so long?"

"Perfect," Carter responded sarcastically. "I'm three minutes late, and you're harassing me?"

"I've gotta keep you in line, Carter."

Charli had dressed for the occasion. She wore a heavy jacket, a scarf wrapped around her neck, and a cowboy hat perched on top of her head like Carter. She hoisted herself onto Midnight, and they were off. The horses seemed to be talking to each other as they snorted in the air pushing out a mist that mixed with the falling snow.

When they got to Dottie B's house, a front porch light was on. They tied their horses to a snow-covered fence. They both took off their hats and shook the snow off. Then they put them back on their heads and started shoveling a path to the front door.

It didn't take long. The snow was white and fluffy, which made the chore easier. When the two kids got to the porch, Mrs. Barbieri had left them some cookies. Nice touch.

Their work was done. They mounted their horses, and Carter pivoted on Whisper to talk to Charli. "Hey, Charli."

"Hey, Carter," she mimicked.

"Charli, do you want to make sure we don't have school tomorrow?"

"And how do we do that?"

"You'll see," he grinned.

Carter and Charli rode their horses to the village. The flakes cascaded down, illuminated by streetlights and store lanterns, made for a magical scene. It was quiet, peaceful, and, most of all, enchanting.

The two friends talked about school, parents, horses, and their lives. Whisper and Midnight seemed to have continued their conversation as well. A plow could be heard in the distance: the only interruption in this magical moment.

Carter looked at Charli, "You know, Charli. This is kind of romantic."

"Stop it, Carter," she smiled.

"I'm just sayin'."

"Carter, don't get weird on me." She took off galloping down the center of the village with Carter sitting on his horse like a goofball. He gave Whisper a light slap to get his horse in motion.

When he finally caught up with her, they trotted to their destination. The place where they could create a situation for 'no school.' It was a beautiful frame colonial at the edge of town. They both were trying to muffle giggles with their gloves as they tied their horses to tree branches weighted down by the snow and out of sight from the house: the superintendent's house.

They waded through the snow carrying their shovels. They got to the back door, where the superintendent of schools would come out to test the snow conditions. The buddies gently dug their shovels into the snow and piled it up against the back door. With the two of them working, their task was completed within minutes. Upon retreating from the house, they used the back of their shovels to smooth out where they had dug as well as their tracks. Hopefully, the falling snow would help conceal their path.

They quietly trotted away. The snow muffled the sound of hooves. When they got a safe distance from the house, they burst out laughing and galloped most of the way home, distancing themselves as fast as they could from the 'scene of the crime.'

Carter escorted Charli to her barn and helped her unsaddle Midnight and wipe him down.

"That was fun, Carter."

"It really was. Thanks for helping out, Charli." He pulled himself up onto Whisper. "We'll see you soon, buddy," and he waved goodbye as his horse trotted down the snow-covered driveway into the darkness.

"We'll see you soon," Charli said softly. As she walked back to her house, she thought about the evening: *It was romantic.* With snow collecting on her hat, she whispered to herself, "Don't get weird, Charli."

~ 14 ~

THE CALL

That Monday morning, the Paw Paw schools had a snow day. Damon had run into the bedroom to tell Carter, who was still sleeping. "Carter! Carter! No school today."

After rolling around in the blankets to face Damon, Carter responds, still cradled by the sandman, "Good. Real good. Now let me go back to sleep." He rolls over on his side, fluffs his pillow, and falls back to sleep.

Damon looks at his brother, covered with blankets. "I thought you'd be happy. It's as if you knew we didn't have school, Carter."

Carter's response was just light snoring.

The faint wail of a siren woke Carter up as his brother burst into his room, screaming, "Dottie B.'s house is on fire. Get up!!!!"

. . . .

The kids were in school the following Wednesday. Emmitt and Rachel were sitting at the kitchen table looking out at the snow-covered farm: the barn, outbuildings, and fences, all wearing a blanket of white.

"We have a lot of work to do still taking care of animals with all this snow. They won't be able to go out for a while. I'll be glad when the kids get back from school to get the hay ready for them and to clean the stalls."

"They're good workers, and that's a lot of work," Rachel replied, sipping her coffee. Just then, the landline phone rang. The Dixon's still couldn't separate themselves from the old way of communicating. Although they had cell phones, the landline gave them a sense of the past, the less hectic days. However, spam calls seemed to inundate their line more than communications from family and friends. Thank goodness for caller I.D.

Rachel looked at the I.D. "It's from the Superintendent of Schools, Emmitt," she said with a curious face.

"Oh! Pick it up, Rachel, and we'll find out what he wants."

"Hello," Rachel said to the receiver. Emmitt could hear the man talking in the background. "Oh, my. Rachel said. Her face became contorted. She responded to the man on the other end, "Yes. We can come in around noon. Thank you, sir."

"What's the deal?" asked Emmitt calmly.

"That was Mr. Mantenuto, the Superintendent. He wants to talk to us as soon as possible.

"Did he say what it was concerning?

"He just said that it involved Carter, and he would like to speak to us in person.

"The Superintendent's office was quite spacious, with a desk for his personal use and a large table with enough room for about six chairs to accommodate larger meetings. However, this was not a large meeting, and Mr. Mantenuto had placed two chairs in front of his desk for the Dixons.

Mrs. Maillet, the secretary, had called the Superintendent on the intercom to let him know the Dixons had arrived. She escorted them to the door opened it. "Mr. Mantenuto is expecting you."

"Thank you," said Rachel nervously, politely.

The Superintendent stood up and walked over to greet them, shaking both their hands and welcoming them to his office. He was not a tall man but very husky with broad shoulders. Town folk had heard he played and coached hockey back in a small New England town. Emmitt had heard that as well. But, looking at the man, Emmitt thought he'd hate to get checked into the boards by that fire hydrant.

"Have a seat right here, folks," he said, pointing to the two chairs he had positioned earlier.

"Thank you," said Emmitt. Rachel smiled her appreciation.

Mr. Mantenuto circled back to his seat behind his desk, sat down, and said, "Thank you for coming in at such short notice. But I wanted to address this situation as soon as possible." Emmitt patiently waited for him to unravel what the situation was. "Your boy, Carter. He's a good boy," Mr. Mantenuto said warmly, trying to set the parents at ease. It didn't work. They were concerned. He continued, "I'll get right to it."

"Please do," said Emmitt respectfully.

"Well. The other night your son and a girl named Charli were seen by one of the men plowing the streets. They had tied their horses to a fence just out of view from my home."

Rachel squirmed in her seat and grasped Emmitt's arm. "Just listen, Rachel," Emmitt said softly and smiled at her.

Mr. Mantenuto continued, "They approached my back door and shoveled snow up against it so that I couldn't get out." He paused to read their expressions. Mrs. Dixon cupped her mouth. Mr. Dixon maintained his composure. "I had to call school off since not getting out of my house is one of the criteria I use to cancel school."

Mr. Dixon spoke, "What is going to happen now?"

"I'm afraid I will have to suspend Carter for three days from school."

"Good," said Mr. Dixon sternly.

"Good?" responded Mr. Mantenuto.

"Yes! Good. Suspend him for a week if you think that would be more appropriate. Carter has got to learn about consequences. What he did was wrong. In his mind, he may have thought it to be innocent, but it was not." Mr. Mantenuto started smiling. This baffled Emmitt. "Why are you smiling, sir?"

"Because usually when I have to talk to parents about punishment for their children, they become defensive and try to justify their child's misdeeds. Not you nor Mrs. Dixon." He looked at Rachel. She smiled back awkwardly.

"I was going to suspend Carter and Charli for a week, but the fire chief told me about circumstances at Dottie B's house. He said that Carter and Charli had dug a path to her house and shoveled out the fire hydrant. Because of them, the firefighters could access the hydrant and get to Dottie B's house quickly before any real damage was done. Dottie even gave them some cookies that weren't burnt by the stove fire."

"Thank you," said Rachel. She was happy that Mr. Mantenuto had seen the good in Carter and in Charli. However, she was worried that his reputation and theirs would be tainted within the community. But that would have never happened. The Dixons were respected in the village of Paw Paw.

Then Emmitt spoke, "But they never should have blocked your back door, sir." He sighed, "Suspend him for a week."

The Superintendent smiled back at the couple, "Three days is more than enough for both Carter and Charli. They're good people. I see where they get it."

~ 15 ~

FACE THE MUSIC

Carter and Charli felt foolish. Although the kids in school thought their shoveling episode was hilarious, they were both embarrassed because they had let down their parents. The Dixons and Rexes didn't bring down the hammer on their children, but they had a stern talk with them in their respective homes. *Do the right thing* was the mantra all the children have been taught. Both Carter and Charli had veered away from that conviction and had to confront the issue head-on.

Carter sat nervously in the reception area of the Superintendent's office. Charli sat with him but not so much nervous as mad: mad at Carter.

"You and your big idea. Why did I even listen to you?"

"Charli, I'm sorry."

"Sorry, doesn't cut it, Carter. Think before you make a decision like that."

Carter wanted to say something like the same thing to her but knew that he had enticed her into shoveling the snow barrier to the Superintendent's door. He was responsible for getting her involved and for the whole thing. It turned out to be a disaster.

Mrs. Maillet couldn't help but overhear their little banter. She said nothing. She has heard a lot worse over the years of being a school secretary. A whole lot worse. Her phone rang.

"Yes! I'll bring them into your office."

The two teenagers glanced at each other, pried themselves from their seats, and followed the secretary to the door. Mr. Mantenuto was sitting at his desk, and he beckoned them into the room. He pointed to the chairs that were placed in front of his desk. It was almost a rerun of the meeting with Mr. and Mrs. Dixon.

"So, Carter and Charli, you wanted to talk with me?"

"Yes, sir," they said simultaneously.

Carter looked at Charli as if asking permission to speak, and he did. "Sir, it was totally my fault. I thought it would be funny to pile snow up to your back door knowing that you would call off school if you couldn't get out." Mr. Mantenuto listened carefully. "Charli, was only there because I asked her to go. It was completely my idea." Charli looked at Carter with wilted admiration. ". . . and I'm sorry to you, to the county and," he turned to face Charli, "and to you, Charli, for dragging you into this mess."

Charli nodded back to him with a half-smile.

The Superintendent spoke, "Carter, I appreciate your apology. However, it does not negate the fact that you did something very wrong." Carter dipped his head in response. "And Charli," She perked up. Her eyes nearly popping out of her head. ". . . you are at fault as well. You have the common sense to determine right from wrong. This was wrong. You simply could have told Carter that you weren't going to do it and walked . . . well, in this case, trotted away."

"Yes, sir." She hung her head in shame, and puddles of water formed in her eyes.

"I'm sorry, Charli," Carter said again and patted her shoulder. She moved away slightly.

"This, my friends, is a lesson learned. Also, the consequences could have been much more severe if it hadn't been for your gestures of kindness by shoveling out a path to Dottie B's door and clearing space around the fire hydrant. Focus on the good things you do from now on and make better decisions in the future."

He got up to escort them out of the office. They stood up as well.

"Thank you, Mr. Mantenuto," they both said.

"Actually, thank you. I know it wasn't easy for you to come in to see me. It shows character."

When Carter and Charli were walking to Emmitt's truck, Charlie had one last comment for Carter, "You're a jerk."

He embarrassingly responded, "You're right," and hung his head as he opened the door for Charli. "You are absolutely right," he whispered.

In the back of his mind, he was worrying that his actions would affect his walk-on status at WMU. His parents had wondered the same thing.

Emmitt decided to be proactive and called Coach Lester. He was relieved when the coach told him it was more of an adolescent prank and not considered an event to rescind the football offer. However, another incident at Western could sideline Carter.

~ 16 ~

LESSONS LEARNED

Carter loved Western's campus. He had walked it many times with his family. He had gone to many games, whether it be a basketball game at Reed Fieldhouse or screaming with the Lawson Crazies as the fans were affectionately called at a hockey game or going to a concert at the Gilmore Theater Complex on campus. Carter, Damon, and Emily enjoyed throwing coins into the fountain plaza as they watched the eight jets shoot water hundreds of feet into the air. Carter admired the aesthetic blend of the old and new architecture, the paths, the greenery complementing the buildings, the fountains on campus. He loved it all. Now he was a student in a place he felt comfortable, at home.

He had to attend early for summer football practices to prepare for the upcoming season. It was great meeting the new players and getting support and tips from the veterans.

He also took a class to alleviate the academic workload during the regular school year. Balancing football and school were not easy for any players but especially for Carter. He struggled. Not that he didn't have the ability. He lacked focus.

Carter's first year on the football team was uneventful. He hardly played at all with the exception of several special team appearances. However, he made an impression on the coaches with his work ethic and football skills.

Coach Lester approached him after one practice toward the end of the football season. "Carter, get ready for next season. You have demonstrated great desire and an elusive skill set for the wide receiver position."

"Thank you, sir," said Carter.

"However, I have been contacted by several of your professors." Carter gulped. They have told me you have been bordering on flunking."

Carter hung his head and muttered his response, "Yes, sir."

"Carter, we will set you up with a tutor to help you in that area."

Carter lifted his head and looked at Coach Lester, "I need it. Thank you."

Carter was assigned a tutor every Tuesday and Thursday evening. He would go to the Waldo Stadium player classrooms. That would make it easy for him to attend the sessions immediately after practice. What didn't make it easy was the tutor was an upper-class coed. A pretty, smiling, intelligent upper-class coed who made it very difficult for Carter to focus . . . at least on his school work.

Her name was Julie. She had blonde hair that dangled down to her shoulders. She was about five foot eight, nicely dressed in jeans, a Vanderbilt sweatshirt with a white collared blouse peeking out the top. Julie also wore circled black glasses perched on her thin nose. She was getting her master's at Western. She had received her undergraduate degree in European Studies from Vanderbilt and was a no-nonsense instructor.

In their first session together, Carter would pretend to listen. He smiled when he responded and just nodded as if he knew he understood. However, when he had to give an answer or write a response, he overthrew the target by yards.

"Carter, you've got to pay attention," Julie urged.

"I know. But I just can't seem to get focused, and I'm tired from practice."

Julie glared sternly at him and barked, "Quit making excuses and get focused."

Carter noticed that Julie's light blue eyes turned to a deep purple when she was mad. Grinning, he thought to himself, she really is pretty even when mad.

Julie noticed he wasn't on the same page, literally and figuratively. She pushed her chair back, stood up, and leaned forward on the table, balancing herself with her outstretched hands. Then, with a stare that would have stopped a bear in its tracks, she sneered, "Get yourself another tutor, Carter." She stood up, pivoted, and walked out the door.

Stunned, Carter leaped from his chair and ran after her. When he caught up to her, he grabbed her by the arm and spun her lightly around. She looked down at his hand on her biceps. "Carter, don't make this ... "

He let go as though he had just touched a hot iron. He took a few steps back. "I'm sorry," he gulped. "I'm sorry for being a jerk." She just looked at him with a blank stare. Then he pleaded with her, "I'm sorry. Please come back. I need your help. I need your skills."

If only it were that easy, she thought. But she liked Carter even though he frustrated her. He was innocent and genuinely needed her help. And quietly, unprofessionally, she thought he was handsome. She felt guilty for harboring such a shallow reason to help him, but it contributed to her returning to the table. The tutoring resumed.

~ 17 ~

GROWING UP

The tutoring helped immensely, and Carter could complete his first year without losing any credits. This accomplishment also enabled him to continue with football. In addition, he and Julie had developed a pleasant tutor/student relationship that carried through to Carter's sophomore year. They had become friends despite the age difference. And they would talk about things other than class work.

"Julie, do you have other siblings?"

"Yes. I do, Carter. I have an older brother, Scott, who is a doctor. I am very proud of him."

"Is he a lot like your father?"

"I suppose. My father passed away from a car accident from losing control on black ice just after I was born." Julie said flatly.

"I'm sorry."

She looked away, lost in thought. "My mother sold the house, bought a small condo, and we lived there together: my mother, my brother and me. They both still live in Nashville.

"Wow! So, you didn't have much."

"Carter, we had each other. Besides, the only thing I wanted was my father. Stuff would never replace him."

Carter didn't know what to say and repeated himself, "I'm so sorry, Julie."

Julie looked up and stared him in the eyes, "Don't be sorry, Carter. Life is full of beatdowns. All you can do is get up and prepare yourself for the next blow."

"Kinda like football."

She looked at Carter sympathetically, "Yah. Kinda like football."

"Do you have a boyfriend, Julie?"

"Wow, Carter. You're getting pretty personal here."

"I guess I am." He repeated the question, though, "Do you have a boyfriend?"

"I think I do?

"What kind of an answer is that?"

"Carter, relationships can be complicated. Two different people are trying to find common ground is challenging. We're all made up of different backgrounds, education, experiences. Our perceptions of how things should be don't always coincide. Nor should they."

Now it was Carter's turn to look away in thought. Then, after a slight pause, "I have a lot to learn, Julie."

"Yes. You do. But learn as much as you can about everything: about religions, cultures, empathy, and people. We're all different, Carter. But in so many ways, we're all the same."

"I don't know if I really understand," he said, a little perplexed.

"I'm not sure I do either, Carter. I'm still trying to figure it out."

Their relationship grew, as did their bond as mentor to student, as friend to friend.

Julie was supportive of his football endeavors and attended a few games when she could. She was allowed on-field access because of her affiliation with the football tutoring program.

On those few occasions when she would go, Carter would run-up to her after the game.

"Thanks for coming, Julie."

"I'm glad I did, Carter. You did well."

"Aw, shucks."

"You got beat down on a couple of plays."

"I sure did, but I got right back up," he smiled.

Julie smiled back, "You sure did. You're learning, Carter."

Then she turned, waved over her shoulder, and walked out of the stadium.'

"Thanks for coming," Carter yelled. She kept walking and waved her hand over her shoulder. "Thanks for coming," he said again quietly.

~ 18 ~

FEELING WOOZY

Carter became very comfortable at Western and with football: a little too comfortable. He had made friends on and off the field some of whom were not of the best influence.

Carter had attended a few parties when his tight schedule allowed such privileges. Football, school, and working the farm were not very accommodating to allowing for free time. However, this night, Carter ended up at an off-campus party. It was in a house on Stuart Ave that had been converted for student living: kegs and all. Carter was not into drinking, but the guys hosting the social event insisted he party like an animal.

"Come on, Carter. Just have one beer. It ain't going to hurt you," coaxed a disheveled party goer.

A pretty coed snuggled up to Carter, "Here, Carter. Have a sip from my glass.

He hesitated, but her blue eyes and smile were too much for him. "OK," he said acquiescing to her charm. He took a sip and looked up, "Not bad."

"I thought you might like it," she smiled.

"Well, actually, I don't like it, but I can tolerate it."

"Here's a solo cup for you, Carter. Now you can fill your own up when needed."

"Thank you. What's your name?" he asked as he filled his cup.

"My name is Allison."

Carter took a sip of beer. Then he extended his hand, "Nice to meet you Allison."

"Real nice to meet you, Carter."

As the night inched by, Carter and Allison got to know each other a little better. And with each tick of the clock, they sipped more beer. By the time Allison had left with her friends, Carter's head was spinning.

"Carter you better get some rest," a voice said that he didn't recognize. "You have practice tomorrow." That is the last thing that Carter remembered from the night until the morning sunlight burned into his eyes.

"Where am I?" he mumbled.

No answer. Carter struggled to sit himself up on the sofa and sat there trying to get his bearings. "What the hell did I do?" His head was still spinning. He noticed the clock on the wall. He was supposed to be at practice for an early session at 8:00 a.m. It was already 8:30 a.m. He wrestled himself up to his feet and almost fell back unto the couch. "I'm in trouble," he muttered and stumbled his way out of the house to Waldo Stadium.

"You're late, Carter," yelled the wide receiver's coach, Chris Chestnut.

"I'm sorry, Coach," he mumbled back.

Coach Lester walked up. "What's going on, Carter? You look a mess." Seeing Carter's blood shot eyes and hearing his slurred speech Lester says,

"Have a tough night, Carter?"

Embarrassed he responded, "Yes, sir."

"Well, you still have to practice. We have a big game this Saturday."

"Yes, sir." Carter just wanted to go home and flop himself onto the bed. That wasn't going to happen.

For half the practice Carter ran pass routes and tried to catch passes from Eleby. The ball constantly slipped through his fingers or eluded him because he stumbled running his routes. He was getting hit on the helmet, his pads, and looked like a drunk giraffe.

The other players ran through their exercises but would glance over occasionally. Some chuckled. Some just stared. No one said anything.

Carter made a few trips to the sidelines to barf. And that's putting it mildly. He drank plenty of water to keep hydrated, but that didn't help how he was feeling. Coach Chestnut turned to Coach Lester, "Do you think he's had enough?"

"Do you?"

They both smiled and said to each other, "Hell, no!"

For the rest of the practice, Carter ran drills with the team, did squats, headed for the sidelines, came back and ran sprints. "I hope he learned his lesson," said Coach Lester to Chestnut.

"We all make mistakes," replied Coach Chestnut. "Let's hope he learns from this."

~ 19 ~

A TONGUE LASHING

Carter sat with Julie going over areas with which he was having problems. Her brother was going to be visiting her and she was excited. However, Carter dampened that enthusiasm. He was a little distant. Julie tried to figure out what was going on.

"Carter, what's wrong. You always smile and you're not the same ole Carter."

"Aw nothin'," he mumbled.

"Come on, Carter. You're not going to learn anything with this attitude."

Carter wiggles around in his seat and then says, "I got drunk last week."

"You got drunk?"

"Well, it wasn't my fault!" he exclaimed defensively.

Julie cocked her head sideways, "Carter, how cannot it be your fault?"

He let out a long gasp of air, "Well, this girl, Ally, or Allison, or something made me drink beer."

"Are you kidding me, Carter?" Julie yelled. You're blaming this on a girl?"

"Yeah. You weren't there. You don't . . ."

Julie interrupted, "Carter, I don't have to be there to tell you that you're a fool."

"What do you mean?"

"Carter, you're blaming someone else for what you had full control of that night," she snarled.

"But, I . . . "

"But nothing! Take ownership, buddy," screams Julie. "Take control of what happens to you: good or bad. That is the only way you'll survive in this world. You blame other people for what is really your fault you'll never improve, you'll never be a better person.

The door opens slightly. Another tutor peeks in, "Is everything OK in here?"

"Yes!" Julie barks. "We're just having some innovative learning."

"OK," he says and the door gently closes.

"Where was I?" Julie asked frustrated.

"Ownership," Carter meekly answers.

"Yeah!! Ownership!" Julie erupts as if launched by a rocket. "Carter, if you blame everything on others like your teachers, your coaches, your parents, your friends, your ADHD, you'll never get better in anything."

"Why wouldn't I?" Carter asks foolishly.

"BECAUSE YOU WON'T CHANGE. YOU WILL BE WAITING FOR THEM TO CHANGE WHEN IT IS YOU THAT HAS TO TAKE CONTROL, NAVIGATE THE WATERS, OWN YOUR MISTAKES. BE THE CAPTAIN OF YOUR SHIP." Julie blares almost in tears.

There's a knock at the door.

"We're fine," Julie yells. "Go away."

The door sways open. A man in a wheelchair guides himself slightly into the room.

"Oh, my," Julie gasps. She jumps from her seat and runs over to the man and hugs him. She turns to Carter smiling, "This is my brother."

The pressure in the room dissipated as soon as Julie looked at her brother. She was engulfed with happiness and, yet, tears streamed down from her eyes. She introduced Carter to Scott, "This is my brother. My brother the doctor," she said with pride.

"Hi, sir," said Carter.

Extending his hand, Julie's brother said, "I'm Scott. Nice to meet you, Carter."

"I didn't know you couldn't walk," Carter said candidly.

"Oh, I forgot I couldn't walk. I'm so used to wheeling myself around. It's just my life."

"When did you get, . . ." Carter pauses and points to the wheelchair, "like that."

"Carter, I'm sure that Julie told you that our father was in an accident and died."

"Yes! She did."

"I was in that same accident and lived. I promised myself that I was going to make the best of my life no matter what."

Julie looked at her brother admiringly, "And you did. And you certainly did. And next time, when I'm in Nashville, we'll go to another Predator hockey game.

~ 20 ~

THE SECRET

Mr. Emmitt was brushing his horse in the stable and glanced out of the open barn doors displaying a beautiful day. He looked at Carter chasing Emily around in the sun by the pig pen. They were laughing. Carter was taunting her by flipping her pigtails. Emily finally ran into the house to escape, and Carter wandered into the barn.

"Oh! Hi Dad."

"Hi Carter. What are you up too!"

"Nothing much. Thought I'd come in here to see if anything needed to get done."

"No, I took care of most of it." He looks at Carter with serious but twinkling eyes. "Have a seat on this box, Carter."

"Sure, Dad," Carter said curiously.

Standing up looking down at Carter, "When were you going to tell me?"

"Tell you what, Dad?"

"You know, Carter. About the drinking."

Carter almost fell off of the box he was sitting on. "Dad!! How did you find out?"

"Carter, it's a small town. News travels easily when distance isn't in the way."

Carter hung his head in shame. He remembered what Julie told him about ownership and not blaming others. He was going to take control of his life by wrapping himself in truth, in integrity. He was going to be the captain of his ship.

He told the entire story to his dad. He even told him about football practice, the wobbly legs, slurring his speech, barfing on the sidelines, and blood shot eyes. This was certainly more information than Mr. Dixon needed, but it was more for Carter to cleanse himself of guilt and to grow as a man. To be the captain of his ship.

Emmitt leaned over and patted his son on the shoulder. "We all make mistakes, son. I've told you that before. We all must learn from them." He looked up around the barn as if his eyes were searching for words.

"Carter, I have something to share with you. Something I'm not very proud of."

Carter looked up at his father like a confused puppy dog. "Yes, dad?"

When I was living here with you guys and your mom, I was a little reckless."

"Reckless?"

"Yes! I was having a few beers down at the pub in the village. I didn't have many, but enough to impede my abilities. I was coming home and passing by Dottie B's house. All of a sudden a deer ran out in front of me." Emmitt pauses. Now it was his turn to hang his head. "Chasing after the dear was Oatmeal, Dottie B's beloved golden." Emmitt takes a deep breath. "Well, I hit Oatmeal and . . . killed him."

"What did you do then, dad."

Emmitt's eyes welled as his mind brought him back to that very moment, "I picked Oatmeal up and cradled him in my arms. I took the long walk which seemed like miles up to Dottie B's front door. I kicked on the door until Dottie B answered it. When she saw Oatmeal, her body began to tremor, and she fell to her knees."

"Dad, I'm sorry. I'm so sorry."

"And you know. Dottie B. forgave me. But . . ."

"But what, Dad?"

". . . but I never forgave myself. I haven't had a drink since. You see. Everyone makes mistakes." Emmitt's body began to shudder. A teardrop rolled down his cheek and fell to the barn floor.

Carter had never seen his father cry. Now it was Carter's turn to comfort his father. He stood up and hugged the man he respected so much. Their forms were silhouetted by the sun streaming through the open door.

~ 21 ~

CHRISTMAS DINNER

Sparkling snow had blanketed the ground and hung delicately onto the tree branches. Inside the Dixon home, the house was adorned with wreaths, green and red, porcelain snowmen, and angels. A manger with the baby Jesus, Mary, and Joseph rested on the fireplace mantle. A few animals nestled inside the structure. Three Wise Men stood just outside, bearing gifts for the King of Kings. Strands of straw strewn around completed the scene. A tree adorned with ornaments, and bright lights with a star resting on top stood tall in the living room corner.

JoDee Messina's Christmas CD was playing softly in the background. Emmitt loved JoDee's voice. It brought him comfort now as did her music when he was stationed in Iraq.

The family was gathered around the dining room table. They had just finished telling what they were grateful for and began eating.

Damon poked a forkful of mashed potatoes and guided it into his mouth. Carter was cutting his chicken, and Mr. and Mrs. Dixon were taking sips from their glasses of water. Emily was looking around at the festive decorations. She focused primarily on the manger scene on top of the mantle. Finally, she twisted back around in her seat, facing everyone, and said, "Hey guys."

The family stopped what they were doing. They were surprised by her announcement and curious about what was next. Utensils were put down, drinking glasses were placed back on the table, and all eyes were on Emily.

"Yes, Emily?" asked Rachel.

"I was wondering?" She hesitated and looked around at everyone nervously, not knowing what kind of response her question would evoke. "I was wondering why we don't go to church?"

"Good question, dear," her mom said gently and took a sip of her water.

"Yeah. Why don't we go to church?" Damon followed. Carter listened intently for the answer. He had a feeling he knew it but wanted confirmation from his parents.

Emmitt just cut his chicken and let Rachel respond, "Well, honey. We're in church every day." Emily gave her a funny look. Rachel continued, "Look outside." They all looked out the window, wondering where this was going. "Isn't it beautiful with the moonlight glistening off of the snow?"

"It really is," said Emily.

"And do you hear the sheep in the barn and a cow mooing?"

"I do," Emily smiled.

"Our manger is here. Our church is here. It is the sky, the moon, the farm. It is in this room. It is this family. It is every family," Rachel said softly.

Emily looked confused, "But why don't we go to church?"

Emmitt entered the conversation, "God believes we are the church as we all bathe in the miracles of His making. To be grateful, to be respectful, to be kind, and aware of the beauty around us is God's wish. Like mom said, we are the church."

"Do you still want to go to church, Emily?" She shrugged her shoulders. Emmitt continued, "Which church do you want to go to?" This was getting interesting; the boys thought as they looked on curiously.

"I don't know?"

"Well, you could be a Baptist, a Catholic, an Evangelical, an Anglican, a Protestant, an Ecumenical, . . ." Emily glanced around at her family as her dad droned on, ". . . a Greek Orthodox. There are also different religions such as Muslim, Jewish, the belief of Buddhism and . . ."

"O.K., Dad," Emily interrupted.

"But the most important thing is not the church you go to nor even the religion one follows. The most important thing is to live your life by always trying to do the right thing. As it says in the bible: Thou shalt love thy neighbor as thyself. Also: let us not love in word, neither in tongue; but in deed and in truth."

"And in English, Dad?" questioned Emily.

"It means treat everyone with love no matter who they are. Also, show your love through how your treat others and always be truthful. We are all God's children no matter what religion or race we are," said dad.

"That makes sense. People should always be truthful and kind anyway," Emily responds satisfied.

"Good answer," smiled Emmitt.

Rachel injects, "God never said you had to go to church or be a certain religion to be a good person. Just do what is right as dad said. Treat everyone respectfully. Don't judge. Look for the good in everyone. You get the idea."

Damon speaks up, "It's not always that easy."

Emmitt finally says, "Doing the right thing is not always easy, son, but it is always the right thing to do." Then, he smiles, ". . . like helping your mom with the dishes."

The CD player had just switched to another disc as he was talking. JoDee Messina's song "That's God" began playing, and the lyrics drifted throughout the room:

"Have you ever stepped outside, felt the sun on your face?
Seen the waters of the ocean reach so far they start to fade?
Have you ever seen a mountain top reach up and kiss the sky?
That's God
Have you ever seen the wonder in the eyes of a child?
Or felt the way the room lights up with that tiny little smile?
Witnessed their amazement at the simplest of things?
That's God"

The family all stopped talking, looked at each other, and listened until the song had finished—profound timing. The point was made.

~ 22 ~

A CALL TO KURDISTAN

In October of 2019, Emmitt walked around the farm with a cloud over his head. His thoughts had drifted to the Middle East with concern about his Kurdish friends, their families, and their safety.

Trump and Defense Secretary Mark T. Esper declared victory over an Islamic caliphate in Syria and Iraq. The withdrawal of American forces from northern Syria was enacted. The approximately 1,000 American troops, mostly Special Operations forces, left quickly.

That withdrawal in Syria and Iraq abandoned Kurds. The people who had saved Emmitt, cared for him, and gave him a home away from home. This left them in harm's way – in the face of oncoming conflicts with the Turks, who historically have seen the Kurds as domestic rebels, if not terrorists.

Emmitt was concerned for his friends. He called Mizgeen and Hemen in Kurdistan to see how they were doing. He was able to get Mizgeen, who said, "Silav hevale min."

"Hello, Mizgeen. Tu cawa yi?" Emmitt responded.

Mizgeen now spoke in English. "I'm fine, my good friend. It is great to hear your voice."

"And yours as well. How are your family and Hemen?"

"We're fine, and Hemen is still crazy." They both laughed.

"Will you be affected by the withdrawal of the American soldiers, Mizgeen?"

"Don't worry about us. We're good. Just take care of yourself and your family, my friend." Mizgeen, Hemen, and their people always dismissed hard times as a problem. Instead, they had accepted them as life. Emmitt was not convinced that they were all doing well, but he felt comfort in Mizgeen's words.

The conversation went on with the two friends, where they shared stories of people they knew, told jokes, and talked about ordinary things that were happening in their lives. When Emmitt hung up, he was greatly relieved. His two friends, his two Muslim friends who had saved him, were all right.

He just hoped that his children realized the importance of friendship like he had with his Kurdish buddies. He hoped that Carter, Damon, and Emily wouldn't discard others because they were different. All he could do was try. After that, it was up to them.

~ 23 ~

DRUNK GIRL

In the Arcadia Grove apartment complex on Lafayette Ave, three girls from the same hometown settled down in their new surroundings. They had grown up in Wellesley, Massachusetts, an affluent town approximately twenty miles west of Boston. They were bright, confident, and pretty.

Seeking a change, they all decided to venture off to the Midwest. Even though they had been accepted to many of the New England colleges such as UMass, Boston University, Bates, and so on, they wanted to experience another area, another lifestyle.

Western Michigan became their collective choice. One girl, Robyn, wanted to become a pilot, and Western had an Aviation Department. Another, Joyce, wanted to get an engineering degree. Western had that as well. The third girl, Kathy, wanted to major in business -- the business of partying.

They had been at WMU for two years and had recently moved out of their dorm, Harrison-Stinson, located in Valley 3. It was a beautiful location with a pond, multiple dorms situated among tall trees, and activities for the residents. They lived in a coed floor assigned by gender. They loved it there but wanted an escape from the antics of dorm life.

Robyn and Joyce decided to get their studies in order. They usually spent much of their time at Waldo Library. It accommodated late night hours with a café. Personalized expert help was available as well as a wide range of space and technologies. Their workload was challenging, and they were determined to do well. But on this night, they were at the apartment.

However, although very competent, Kathy wanted a break from boxes and books. She had met some boys at the climbing wall at Western's recreation center a few days earlier. She had planned to meet them at a local bar across the street from Waldo Stadium.

Kathy put on worn jeans, sneakers, and a cute peek-a-boo top, which revealed enough to draw some attention for the occasion.

As Kathy gathered her purse, Joyce said, "Have fun."

"Oh, I will," Kathy responded with a caucus laugh.

Robyn spoke, "Be careful, Kathy." She then motioned with her hand to her mouth as if taking a drink.

Kathy laughed again, "Don't worry about me. I can take care of myself." Robyn and Joyce simply looked at each other and shrugged. "Bye. I'll see you when I get home . . . whenever that is?"

. . . .

Charli decided to attend Western and was enjoying her experience. She became the rider of the horse, the Bronco mascot, before the football games and frequently would come with Carter. After all, they had to bring the mount, which was Whisper, in the horse trailer.

She loved the excitement of the games and got a chance to do what she liked best: ride a horse. Whisper was perfect for the job since he was so mild and not spooked by the crowd noise. They both loved having the fans take pictures of them during the festivities. Soon, they would make their way through the tunnel and the team would gather behind them. After the announcement of the Bronco football team, the players burst out onto the field lead by Coach Lester, with Charli and Whisper leading the charge.

Carter had just finished an afternoon practice. He got a text from Charli, who had just gotten out of a class on campus, asking if he would like to go to the University Roadhouse for some food before heading home.

She was using Carter's dad's truck. She had dropped him off at practice earlier in the day. When she got there, Carter was sitting with Jerry Collins, a linebacker on the team. Jerry was not only a talented player but also a gifted singer. He was president of The A Cappella Project, a co-ed non-competitive a cappella group. He was the first black student to hold that position. His girlfriend, Erica, had joined him. They made a nice bi-racial couple; both were attractive and carried themselves with confidence.

Charli had never met either of them. Carter introduced Charli to Jerry and Erica. They hit it off and became entrenched in their socializing from the start. So much so that they were oblivious to others in the bar/restaurant.

A girl had had a little too much to drink at the bar. OK. A lot to drink. She seemed to be loaded. The bartender had cut her off from drinking any more beers, but she was accompanied by two guys pushing their drinks in her direction.

One of the guys said, "So, Kathy, what do you want to do after we finish here?"

"I doon't . . . knowwa." She slurred her words loudly and had trouble keeping her balance.

The other, shorter man said, "Well, why don't we all go back to our apartment, and we'll take it from there." He turned and winked at his buddy, who nodded back.

"Thaat... sooounds... liiike a gooda ideea," Kathy cackled.

The three were so loud that those in the restaurant couldn't help but overhear. Carter had seen Jerry's eyes squint with concern. Jerry was sitting facing the bar and had a clear view of the activity. The girls could see as well. Carter had turned around to watch.

The interaction between Kathy and the guys continued. "Well, come on, Kathy. Let's go," said the shorter man.

"Lettt... meeea.... haavva... one mooore...."

Kathy never finished her sentence. Instead, she noticed a blurred figure standing next to her. "Time to go, Kathy," said Carter calmly.

"Hey, she's with us," blurted the taller of the two guys and stepped menacingly closer to Carter.

The smaller one barks, "You guys already have girls." He peered at Jerry, Erica, and Charli. They were looking at the scene with concern from their table.

"She's my sister, and she has had enough to drink. Come on, sis," Carter said to Kathy, gently holding her arm. "We've got to get home."

Kathy looked up from her leaning position at the bar. "Siista? Yooora... cute."

Carter looked at her companions, "She always says that to me when she's had too much." He again said, "Let's go, Kathy."

She smiled at him and blabbered, "Yeahhh... braaotha. Leets ... gooa."

Carter guided her to the table he had been sitting at, leaving the two dudes behind flabbergasted. They began to follow him but had a second thoughts when all two hundred pounds of six-foot four Jerry rose up from his chair. They backed up to the bar, turned, and ordered two more beers.

Carter introduced Kathy to his friends. Her eyes seemed to roll in her head, and she nodded like a floppy dog.

"What are you going to do with . . . her . . . ," Charli began to ask and then corrected herself, ". . . with your sister?"

"Take her to her home," Carter said calmly.

The four friends guided her out the door and headed for Carter's truck. He asked, "Where do you live, Kathy?" At this point, she could barely walk, let alone utter anything of relevance.

"What are you going to do?" asked Jerry, with Erica holding on to his massive arm as she stood beside him.

"I'm not sure," Carter said, examining possible solutions. But, then, he thoughtfully repeated, "I'm just not sure."

~ 24 ~

THE STRANGER

Carter and Charli sat in the F-150 Ford on the way home with Kathy sandwiched between them. Her head bobbled around with every turn.

"I can't take her to my house, Carter. My parents would kill me," insisted Charli."

"I'm sorry, Charli. I should never have even asked you. Unfortunately, it was my decision, and I have to deal with it."

"What are you going to do?"

It looks like the Dixon family is going to have an overnight guest.

After dropping Charli at her home, Carter shook his head, looked at Kathy's limp body slumped on the passenger seat, and said, "What have I done?"

He arrived at the farm. He tried to lift Kathy out of the truck but struggled. Even though she was small, she weighed a ton. He nearly dragged her into the house into the living room. She seemed to pop out of her coma. She muttered, "Wheeraa . . . ammm . . . Iyee?"

As soon as she finished her sentence, she flopped onto the sofa. She was out. Carter lifted her legs onto the couch, put a blanket over her, and gently said, "Sleep well, Kathy." She turned on her side and groaned. Yes. She was out . . . out like a light.

"The family was sleeping. Carter left a note on the kitchen table explaining the presence of their guest:

Hi family,
You will find a girl sleeping on the sofa when
you get up. She had had a little too much to drink.
I decided to help her out. She couldn't remember where
she lived, so I brought "my sister" home to sleep it off.
Sorry for any convenience. By the way, her name is Kathy.
I'll explain the rest tomorrow.
Love, Carter

Emmitt and Rachel got up at about the same time. They stretched and cleaned up, gave each other a good morning hug, but said little. However, that changed when they walked out of their bedroom and into the living room. A strange girl, whom they had never seen before, was sleeping on the sofa, snoring like an old dog. Carter's parents exchanged quizzical looks and quietly headed to the kitchen.

"Who the heck is she?" asked Rachel.

"Darned if I know," said Emmitt as he shrugged his shoulders. When the words came out of his mouth, they both noticed the note on the kitchen table.

After reading it, Rachel looked up at Emmitt and said, "Well, there's the answer."

"Our boy. What are we going to do?" Emmitt questioned.

"Well, I'm going to make breakfast. Kathy must be hungry."

"Good idea, Rachel."

Mrs. Dixon began cooking eggs and bacon, put on some coffee, and griddled some pancakes to mix it up a little. The aroma from the fixings traveled throughout the house. Kathy stirred from her sleep aroused by the smell of coffee and the hissing of eggs on the grill.

When she opened her eyes to try to focus, she noticed a girl kneeling in front of her staring. "Who are you?" Emily asked.

Then Kathy elevated her body on one elbow and looked around. Her head was still spinning. Finally, she looked at the strange girl and returned the question, "Who are you?"

"I'm Emily. I live here."

"Hi, Emily. Could you help me up?" Kathy reached out her hand. Emily stood up, grabbed it, and pulled the stranger up to her feet.

When Kathy was standing, she put her arms out to steady herself. At that time, Mr. and Mrs. Dixon walked into the living room after hearing voices.

Kathy looked confused . . . and hungover. The family escorted her to the kitchen table, where they chatted and ate breakfast. The stranger told them about how nice Carter was protecting her and how the girl he was with also was very kind in helping her out. From that point on, she lost track of the events.

Rachel handed Kathy the note that Carter had written. She read it and gasped, "I'm so embarrassed."

Rachel patted her the back of her hand and said, 'We've all had embarrassing moments, Kathy. Every one of us."

In the truck, Carter drove Kathy back to her apartment. The ride was beautiful, with the Paw Paw landscape beckoning to them at every turn. Spacious green fields, maple, and oak trees adorned with yellow, red, and orange leaves, cows in the pasture expressed a sense of serenity. Carter talked very little and occasionally responded to Kathy. His mind was getting this girl back to her apartment and then heading to football practice at Waldo Stadium.

Kathy, however, kept rambling on about how sorry and how embarrassed she was. She continually gushed about how sweet Carter was to take care of her and his family. He smiled his replies to her.

They finally reached her apartment. Kathy looked at Carter before she exited the truck and thought to herself, *he is sooooo handsome.*

"Carter, thank you. You are so very kind and thoughtful," Kathy swooned.

"No problem," Carter said flatly.

Then Kathy slid closer to him, leaned over, and kissed him on the cheek. She then abruptly pulled back, opened the door, and hopped out. She turned and gave Carter a charming smile and waved goodbye delicately with her fingers.

Robyn and Joyce were staring out the window and said, "Oh, boy."

As Carter was driving away, he said to himself the same thing, "Oh, boy." He followed that up with, "Yikes."

~ 25 ~

"INDIVISIBLE AND JUSTICE FOR ALL"

The country was embroiled in a myriad of controversies: A black man, George Floyd, had been killed by police which sparked protests throughout America and riots erupted; the Covid virus was ravaging families and backlash about wearing masks and getting vaccinations cropped up in towns throughout the country; rules were imposed by the government about shutdowns of businesses to prevent the spread of the virus.

Tensions were high among townspeople who were entrenched with their political leanings. This was not a time of domestic tranquility and folks had to be careful what they said about sensitive topics to their friends and even family. A wrong opinion could spark conflict.

Emmitt simplified his emotions as he always did. Do what is right, be thoughtful, and be kind to others. Oh, sure, he had his opinions but they were just that, his opinions, and he was not going to coerce them onto other folks.

Fighting for America made Emmitt more sensitive to the freedoms and the responsibilities of freedoms. He knew there were bad apples in every group. Those police needed to be tried just like the former cop in Kalamazoo who had murdered his wife. However, Emmitt was grateful for all the men and women in blue and was forever grateful to them for risking their lives for them.

He was disturbed by those few who tarnished the badge and the heroics of the police. He felt the same as when a teacher exploits the innocence of a student or a minister who steals money from his parishioners or a soldier who commits atrocities in war. The actions of a few can paint a broad brush of doubt and criticism on an entire group who do good for so many.

He believed in peaceful protests, but the riots bothered him. Emmitt wanted all those who destroyed property, stole from stores and intimidated law enforcement to be punished. They twisted the sincere intentions of those protesting as an excuse to rob, to destroy.

As far as vaccinations and masks were concerned, Rachel and he followed the recommendations of their doctors and of Rachel who worked at the hospital. She told him about patients in the ICU who suffered their final days gasping for breath. They did not want any member of their family to suffer this type of agonizing illness. As far as others deciding what to do: it was their business. They both hoped others would be fine, but their decisions were for their family. What others decided to do was their choice, and the Dixons felt they had no right to impose their feelings upon them.

Emily came home from school, stomped into the living room, and threw her books down.

Rachel and Emmitt had been sitting watching the local news and looked up. "What's wrong, honey," Rachel said.

"I'm sick of wearing this stupid mask." She pulled it out of her pocket and threw it to the floor.

Emmitt stood up, walked beside her and put his arm around her shoulder. "So are we, Sweetheart. But we just want to be safe. Until we hear from people who know, we . . ."

Emily walks away and lands her bottom onto the couch. "Who knows? When will that be?"

Emmitt shuffles over to her and takes a seat beside her. "This virus is complicated. We have to be patient. Time will tell," he softly said.

"Well, I'm sick of it."

"So am I," a voice from the kitchen yells. Damon had come into the house from school. "But what are you going to do? Whine about it? Complain? It's just a mask, for crying out loud."

"I couldn't have said it better," smiles Emmitt.

~ 26 ~

THE 2020 ELECTION

It was the summer of 2020. Carter had conditioned himself for his final year of football at Western. Charli was excited to be riding Whisper again leading the team out onto the field.

But the state was consumed with more things than football. The upcoming election between incumbent Donald Trump and challenger Joe Biden was entangled in controversy. The Republicans were taking political shots at Biden, and the Democrats were taking political shots at Republicans. Both sides were jockeying for votes citing all the reasons why the other candidate shouldn't be elected. It wasn't pretty.

At the evening Sunday meal, the talk was all about the election and Trump versus Biden. "Who should I vote for?" asked Emily.

"Wow! It seems like we just had this discussion. But that was four years ago," said Carter, "and with different candidates."

Mr. Dixon repeated the basics of his talk years ago, "Vote for the person with the most integrity. A man who is kind, empathetic, and concerned about the people, the police, the farmers, . . . about the country."

"And who is that, dad," Damon said leaning on his elbows.

"Take your elbows off the table, Damon," smiled Rachel.

"Right, mom. Sorry," He turned his face toward Mr. Emmitt. "So, who do you think we should vote for?"

Every one leaned forward to hear the answer. "Emmitt finished chewing his string beans, took a drink of water and said with a grin, "Do the research, learn about the platforms and policies of each candidate, find out about their accomplishments and, finally, vote for the man with the most integrity." He speared his fork into a few beans and took another bite.

After dinner he went off to do some of his errands. He stacked some boxes filled with vegetables and used clothing and drove down the driveway. He mumbled to himself as he took a right onto the road. "The one with the most integrity."

~ 27 ~

THE HIGHLIGHT REEL

The season had gone well for Western in this abbreviated season. It was cut short because of Covid restrictions with only six games. The Broncos had won three games in a row. Winning this game against Northern Illinois University at home could give them the momentum to go all the way.

It was a beautiful fall day in October for the upcoming game at Waldo Stadium. The band had marched down from campus as usual with a trail of students following from behind. As they got closer to the Stadium Western's fight song echoed through the air. The fanfare marched passed by Charli who was riding Whisper. Cell phones were being held up by fans filming all the pomp and circumstance unfolding before the game.

When the band marched through the tunnel, Charli trotted Whisper to the opening of the tunnel leading out to the field. In front of her, the cheerleaders and the dance team formed a path. Once the football players and coaches, had grouped behind Whisper, Coach Lester waved his hand forward which launched a sea of athletes. Whisper galloping onto the field and the fans stood and cheered on the team.

Northern Illinois came to play. They were a tough, competitive bunch, and the Broncos had struggled all game to get their offense in gear. Time was not in their favor as the fourth quarter minutes ticked away.

Only five minutes remained. Western was trailing the Huskies 27 to 24. The Broncos defense had just recovered a kickoff runback by Northern Illinois when Keni-Lovely hammered the returner. The ball dropped to the ground and was smothered by a wave Brown and Gold shirts. Western had three minutes to cover 35 yards and score a touchdown.

Kaleb Eleby, the young QB, masterfully guided his team down to the ten yard line with strikes to standout receiver, Skyy Moore, and the big tight end, Brett Borske. However, there were only two seconds left on the clock after the Broncos called a timeout. When play resumed, Eleby stepped back in the pocket. He looked for an open receiver. No one. Moore was doubled team, and Borske slipped.

Kaleb was eventually flushed out of the pocket and scrambled for his life. Out of the corner of his eye, he saw Dixon dash for a speck of open turf. Eleby hit him with a dart. Carter grabbed the ball. NIU players surrounded him. He cut to the right. Then Carter dug his foot into the turf to abruptly change directions. Two Huskie players converged on him, but he spun out of their grasps.

He had two yards to go with only one man to beat. Carter had to go either through him or over him. Carter leaped into the air. The defender stood up and reached around to tackle him. Dixon's right foot crashed against the cornerback's face mask, and he crumbled backwards like a bag of chips.

Carter tumbled into the end-zone. The crowd erupted as the score ended with the Broncos winning, 30 to 27. Carter stood up, handed the ball to the referee, and glanced at the player he had just knocked over. He jogged up to him and knelt beside him. The player, Jim Ebert, the strong safety, was seeing stars. Carter put his hand on the player's shoulder pad to comfort him. Coaches ran out with trainers. Eventually, they carried the injured player off the field. Carter walked off with him and his NIU teammates as fans poured out of the stands onto the field.

~ 28 ~

APARTMENT FANS

That night Kathy, Joyce, and Robyn were sitting in their rental's living room, munching on pizza and sipping wine. They decided to watch ESPN's top ten plays since Kathy had heard about some exciting play during the Western/Northern Illinois game that would be featured.

"So why are we watching this?" asked Joyce.

"I heard there would be something about Western's game on it," Kathy responded. Robyn took a sip of her wine, as did Joyce. They could care less. However, Kathy loved sports, parties, and guys.

The ESPN show began with a countdown of the best plays of the day from any and all sports. There were incredible saves from soccer games, golf shots that dropped into the hole from 50 yards away, diving catches in the end zone and, finally, the play featuring Western Michigan.

Robin Hook, the voice of the Broncos, was doing the play by play. ". . . and Eleby finds Dixon in a sliver of open space. Oh, my. Dixon makes a cut to elude a tackler. Two Northern players wrap him up." Hook's voice vibrates with excitement. "Dixon spins free and now only has one player to beat. He hurdles him. Yes! He hurdles him. His foot slams the player in the face. Dixon stumbles into the end zone for the win!!

Dixon is checking on the player he ran over. He's taking off his helmet and talking with the injured Husky defenseman, Jim Ebert." Finally, the camera closes in on Carter's face. "What a show of sportsmanship and..."

The rest of Hook's play by play was muffled by Kathy screaming as she hopped up from the couch and ran up to the TV, "That's him!!!"

"That's who?" blurted Joyce trying to be overheard by Kathy.

"That's the one who took care of me the other night!"

The girls leaned forward, staring at Kathy's back, obstructing their view. "Kathy, move out of the way, please." Joyce insisted.

"Oops! Sorry." She moved to the side so her roommates could see Kathy's hero.

It was a great shot of Carter. He looked like a gladiator with sweat dripping down his stern, concerned face trying to comfort his downed opponent.

"He's handsome," said Joyce.

"He really is," contributed Robyn.

Kathy stared at the TV and grinned like a Cheshire cat. Then she looked back at the girls. "That's the guy I'm going to marry."

Joyce and Robyn looked at each other and were thinking the same thing: *Good luck to him.*

Carter was interviewed via zoom by ESPN not so much for his spectacular touchdown but for his sportsmanship and empathy for the Northern player, Jim Ebert, who had been injured. During the interview, Carter responded in his humble manner when Mark Sweeney, the host, had told him that he was an example for all athletes: "Aw, Shucks."

Sweeney turned to the camera to make his closing comment, "Let's hope that more players in all sports have an 'aw shucks' moment like Western Michigan's Carter Dixon."

Little did Carter know, but his high light was played over and over throughout high schools and colleges across the country.

....

After the football season, Carter sat down in the family room with his mom and dad. He had some thoughts about his future and wanted to share them with his parents as well as to get some feedback.

He spoke, "I was thinking of going away after this school year at Western."

"What do you mean; going away?" asked his mother in a shocking voice.

"Honey, let him talk," Emmitt said gently.

Carter continued, "I was thinking of entering the football transfer portal and..."

"Sounds dangerous," gasped Rachel who is usually calm, cool and collective. She didn't want her first born to leave the nest.

Emmitt glared at her, "Honey, please let him talk."

Carter continues, "... the transfer portal is where I enter my name into a college football recruiting pool. This allows colleges throughout the nation to see which current college football players want to transfer to another school. Those colleges look for players that fit their needs."

Now Emmitt was curious, "How does it work?"

"Well, I can go to any college that wants me and play football. By doing so, I can get my masters paid for?

"That sounds like a great idea. You'll be able to get a further degree for free." He thought about what he just said and rephrased it, "I mean you'll have to work you're butt off on the field, but you'll be able to get your degree as well? Where will you go?"

"I'm not sure. It all depends on who is interested in me, if any, and if I can qualify."

Rachel pipes in, "I will miss you terribly." Realizing herself sounding hysterical, she attempts to cushion her message, "but you will meet new people, make new friends, experience a different school and environment. It sounds like a great thing."

Emmitt looked at Rachel, "I'm impressed, Rachel. So, you're saying that you're willing to let Carter go away?"

"Reluctantly, yes," she said with a sad face.

One month later, Carter had been contacted by several schools, all of which appealed to him. However, he had never been out east, seen the ocean or traveled in a plane. He decided on Boston College.

When he told his parents his father grinned, "I heard the lobstaw is great."

Carter smiled back, "I heard it was wicked awesome."

~ 29 ~

THE 2020 PRESIDENTIAL RESULTS

The election was on November 2, 2020. The results were in on November 3. Biden had won by 237 electoral votes compared to Trump's 217. He also won the popular vote receiving over seven million votes more than the former president. Biden was now the president... or so it seemed.

Trump and his supporters claimed that the election was rigged and sent a team of lawyers to critical states in an attempt to overthrow the election. They lost sixty-three lawsuits in an effort to unseat Biden as the President.

Emmitt was glad that efforts to verify the election were taking place. Republican governors had recounted the votes. Georgia had three recounts. Republican commissions were formed to investigate any possibility of fraud. None of these groups found any significant abnormalities in the ballots. This made Emmitt feel good knowing that extensive steps were enacted by the Republicans that verified that the election was secure.

However, Trump kept beating the drum of a stolen election. All the results from recounts, investigative commissions, and legal actions that proved the election was secure didn't seem to matter to him nor to his followers. The threads of doubt had been and continued to be woven tightly into the fabric of democracy.

The official stamp of approval for the electoral votes was to occur on January 6, when all the legislators met at the Capitol to verify the votes.

Coinciding with the vote, Trump held a rally of his supporters outside the capital, protesting the election. The emphasis was that Biden was not the president and that Trump was. Speaker after speaker made this charge, and the crowd's emotions amped up.

Trump urged his supporters to walk to the Capitol to convince the Congressional members to delay the electoral vote that would affirm Biden's presidency. Trump said, "We're trying to give them the kind of pride and boldness that they need to take back our country. So, let's walk down Pennsylvania Avenue."

The protesters did just that: they headed for the Capitol. But, unfortunately, the peaceful protest morphed into something far from that: a riot, and it was far from peaceful.

Carter had just come home from classes at Western. He stepped into the kitchen and heard his mother and father talking in louder voices than usual.

Rachel attempted to calm Emmitt down, "Honey, there is nothing you can do. Try to relax."

"This is nuts!" Emmitt groaned. "That is the United States Capitol, and look what they're doing!!"

Carter had walked into the living room. He then stared at the TV in silence. What was on the screen looked like a scene from a movie. People were charging the Capitol with American, Rebel, and Trump flags. Others were using the flag poles as weapons. Everyone was screaming wildly.

One of the men in the crowd threw a fire extinguisher at a policeman's head. Another man jabbed an officer with a flag pole and started to beat him. Other people were breaking windows and attempting to climb into the Capitol.

"What's going on?" Carter asked with great concern for what he was viewing on the screen and concern for his parents. They were both deeply affected by what they were watching.

"Look at this shit," his father yelled. Carter had never heard his father swear before. It made him uncomfortable and nervous. It made him scared.

Carter sat on the sofa's armrest beside his father and patted him on the back. Rachel had her hand resting on Emmitt's shoulder. All three glued their eyes to the screen, the images, the chaos.

Finally, Emmitt broke the heavy silence between the three of them. "I did not go to war for this," he gasped, trying to take in some air.

Emmitt loved this country. He fought for America, its freedoms, the people, and his neighbors. He loved democracy and believed in elections and the constitution's sanctity.

Sirens screamed in the distance before the ambulance arrived at the Dixon farm.

~ 30 ~

THREE WISE MEN

Carter and his mother entered the hospital room. They were surprised to see three men standing around Emmitt's bed. They all turned to face them when they had heard the door open. Two of men had on casual dress clothes. However, one was dressed in a black clergy shirt and a clerical collar. Both Mrs. Dixon and Carter were concerned by the presence of these three men wondering if Emmitt was going to make it.

The man wearing the clerical collar saw the distress etched in their faces and spoke up, "Hello, I'm Father Flynn." He turned and introduced the other two gentlemen. "This is Rabbi Cohen and this is Reverend Tucker." The Rabbi was very distinguished and could have passed for a doctor. Reverend Tucker was a well-built black man with a gentle face. He looked like he could play running back for North Carolina.

"Hello," said Rachel cautiously. She knew the three gentlemen, but was worried as to their presence here, in the hospital, in Emmitt's room. "What are you all doing here? Is Emmitt going to make it?"

Rabbi Cohen replied, "Yes, he is just resting. We had come to visit our friend and check in to see how he was doing."

"Yes," smiled Reverend Tucker, "and we're glad he is doing so well. We had just talked to him, and Emmitt said that he was tired. He closed his eyes and is snoring quietly now."

Father Tucker then said, "We won't take up any of your time with Emmitt." and gestured for the others to go as he took a few steps toward the door.

"Please wait!" sputtered Carter "How do you know my father? Why would you take the time to come here to visit him?" Rachel kept quiet.

"We thought you would know," said the Rabbi puzzled.

"Know what?" Carter responded even more perplexed. He turned to his mom. "What's going on here?"

His mom smiled at her son, "I'll let these gentlemen explain."

"So, you're putting us on the spot, Rachel?" said Father Flynn smiling.

"I didn't mean to, but you would explain it better than me. You know how Emmitt liked to be humble about such things."

"About what things?" asked Carter even more confused.

"Well," began the Rabbi, "you have a very thoughtful, giving, complex man as a father."

"I agree," said Carter. Rachel smiled and nodded.

"Every week he would come to the Temple or Catholic Church or to the Protestant church and bring food for our members," said Rabbi Cohen.

"That's certainly something dad would do." said Carter.

Reverend Tucker now spoke, "And that is not the only thing he would do. He would drive some of the folks to doctor's appointments or to pick up things at the store if they couldn't do it on their own."

Father Flynn injected, "And once a month he stopped by the police and fire departments to bring them goodies."

"Were those goodies the cakes and cookies you made, mom, that we never got to eat?" She smiled her response. "You never told us about those things," said Carter. "Dad never told us."

Rachel looked at her son, "Dad would never talk about what he did for others. He felt people's deeds were more powerful than words. Folks should just help." Carter nodded his head in understanding.

Rabbi Cohen interjected, "He enjoyed talking with people of diversified backgrounds. He told me once that everyone was the same: they loved their families, were grateful for what they had, and that most were good people. Then he would say 'except for a few bad apples' that darkened religions' good.

Suddenly, Emmitt rolled over in his bed and grumbled, "Can't you all keep it quiet in here. I'm trying to sleep. Besides, your pouring it on pretty heavy."

A collective chuckle rose from the group. "OK. We're leaving now," said Reverend Tucker. The three men wished Emmitt the best, turned and shuffled out the door.

Carter turned to his father and said, "Dad, why didn't you tell us about all of this?"

"Why would I? You don't make announcements when helping others. You just do it. Besides, I was just doing my errands."

~ 31 ~

LIFE IS PRECIOUS

Carter was standing by the window when the nurse came into the hospital room. She smiled at him and went directly to Emmitt. She spoke with a cheery voice, "Hi, Mr. Dixon. How are you doing?"

She began to remove the tubes from his father's arm and then the devices attached to his chest. "I'm doing fine," he responded with a raspy voice.

"Well, you look fine," she smiled.

"I'm married," he joked.

"And she is beautiful." The nurse looked at Rachel, who was sitting on the bed's opposite side.

"Thank you,' Rachel said demurely.

"Well, today you are going home, Mr. Dixon. Your heart seems stronger, and you'll be healthy as a horse in time with rest and medication."

"Good! I'm ready."

"You might be ready, but you'll have to take it easy, as I just said. Also, you'll have to take your heart medication as directed."

"Don't worry about me. I'll be fine. Let's get going." His abruptness caught Carter and Rachel off guard. Emmitt was usually courteous and grateful.

"I'm going to get all the paperwork together," said the nurse. "Your family can help you get dressed while I'm gone." She turned to Carter. "And Carter, you can go home as well. It was nice of you to stay here with your father all that time."

"I'm glad we're going home. Hospital food doesn't taste like mom's cooking," said Carter. His mom smiled and softly squeezed Emmitt's hand.

Emmitt looked at Carter when the nurse left, "She's cute!" Rachel had gotten up and retrieved her husband's clothing from the closet shaking her head at his comment.

"Dad, knock it off."

"I'm just trying to be helpful, son."

"Thanks, but no thanks, Dad."

"Here you go, Emmitt," said Rachell gleefully as she held up Emmitt's pair of overalls. "It's official. You're going home!"

~ 32 ~

OBSESSED

Carter and the family were very concerned about Emmitt. They worried about his physical health and his mental state even more. Since coming home, he had to take it easy. However, he spent most of his days plunked on the sofa watching cable news: MSNBC, CNN, but mostly FOX. His demeanor had changed. Each passing day he seemed to get angrier and angrier.

He was happy when he was out working the farm, herding the cattle, or feeding the pigs. The combination of having to rest from his heart problem and his obsession with the attack on the Capitol wasn't good for him. He was becoming a different man. Watching the news was like a bad drug.

One day when Carter arrived home from school, Emmitt was seated on the sofa, now his traditional spot. Carter sat down beside him and said, "Dad, I think . . ." His father just kept watching the TV. Carter tried again, "Dad, I'd like . . ." Seeing he wasn't getting anywhere, Carter grabbed the remote and shut the TV off.

"Hey! What are you doing?" snarled his father.

"Dad. You've got to get out of this funk. You're drifting away from us all."

"What do you expect me to do?" he grumbled.

Carter stood up, stared his father in the face, and said sternly, "I expect you to act like a father, a husband, and a MAN." Then, he turned abruptly and bolted out of the house to the barn.

Emmitt sat stupefied and in disbelief that his son, Carter, would talk to him like that. However, it didn't seem to register. He boiled with anger.

. . . .

Several days later, Mr. Rex came over to visit Emmitt. He parked his truck outside the barn. Carter was feeding the horses, saw Mr. Rex, and came out to greet him.

"Hi, Mr. Rex. Thank you for coming over to see Dad."

I'm more than happy to talk to him. I'll see what I can do to help him get out of his . . . what did you call it . . . his funk?"

Yes," Carter smiled.

"See you in a bit." He walked inside, said hello to Rachel, who was in the kitchen, and went into the living room to see Emmitt.

He was only there for about ten minutes when shouting erupted from the living room.

When Mr. Rex popped out the kitchen door, Carter was still outside. He smiled at Carter, "He'll be fine. By the way, I have something in the back of the truck to . . . to take his mind off of things."

He walked to the bed of the truck and pulled out a cage. He opened it and handed Carter the cutest, fluffiest puppy he had ever seen. "Oh, my. Where did you get this little guy?"

"Charli's cousin's mother's aunt's dog had puppies."

Carter couldn't figure out the sequence of relatives, but it didn't matter. That dog was cute and sweet and just curled up in his arms.

"Bring him to your father and rest it in his arms. That little fellow will help him get his mind straight," smiled Mr. Rex.

Carter cradled the dog in his arms. When he passed his mom in the kitchen, her face transformed from worried to happy.

"Ohhh. He's so cute."

"Mr. Rex brought him for dad to keep his mind off wherever his mind was."

"It might help," Rachel whispered hopefully.

When Carter entered the living room, Emmitt was banging on the side of the TV and playing with the channels.

"What's wrong?" inquired Carter innocently.

"What's wrong?" Emmitt snarled. "I'll tell you what's wrong. That so called a friend of mine, Rexy, disabled my cable connections. So now I can only get local stations."

"That's too bad," commented Carter sarcastically.

His father turned and said, "Now, don't you get smug with . . ." Noticing the dog, "Where did you get that little guy?"

"Sit on the sofa, Dad, and I'll let you hold him."

Mr. Dixon obeyed and sat down. Carter handed him the soft bundle of joy. Emmitt's heart melted.

"What are you going to call him, Dad?"

"What am I going to call him?"

"Yeah. He's your pup. Mr. Rex brought him for you."

"I guess my buddy, Rick Rex, isn't that bad after all." Emmitt looked at the puppy, snuggled him, and then looked up at Carter. His mom, by that time, had come out to the living room and stood beside him. "I'm going to call him Oatmeal. That will make Dottie B. happy." He looks down at the dog, now licking his hand. "You will make us all happy, Oatmeal."

If only it were that easy.

~ 33 ~

THE BREAK THROUGH

Oatmeal followed Emmitt like the pup was hitched to his leg. That fury dog was his buddy. In fact, he was Emmitt's best buddy. The little puppy helped Emmitt to become more grounded, more tolerable. However, Emmitt still was not his old self. As his physical strength improved, so did his mental state. Being on the farm with the horses and other animals heightened his spirit. Also, the cable connection had never been reinstalled. Local news dominated the information and was perfect. It stuck with that: News. Now, his mind was free of conspiracy theories and extreme opinions that bordered on the ridiculous.

Carter was having second thoughts about going to Boston College. He loved the farm, the Paw Paw village, Kalamazoo, and felt comfortable at Western and with the Bronco football team.

He was concerned about his father's health. Although he wasn't a mama's boy, he sure did love his mama. He was closer to Damon and Emily than he ever realized. The thought of being away from them and his parents pulled at his heart. And he would miss Charli, his very best friend.

Leaving all of this seemed to outweigh going eight hundred fifty-five miles to Boston. He didn't know anybody there, wasn't familiar with the coaches or team members, navigating the big city was intimidating, and he wasn't sure how he'd fit in at Boston College. He was a farm boy, plain and simple. They were not.

At dinner time, Carter broke the news after their grateful prayers, "Hey, folks. I have a thought I'd like to share with you," he said thoughtfully. Then, sensing the gravity of his voice, everyone stopped shoveling food into their mouths, drinking water, or playing with their napkins.

Emmitt looked at Carter and said, "Go ahead, son. We're all listening."

Carter fumbled, "Well, I . . . I was thinking . . ."

Rachel leaned over and patted his shoulder, "Go ahead, Carter. What is it?" Damon reached for his glass of water for a sip.

Without hesitating any more, Carter said, "I'm thinking of . . . of not going to Boston College."

The announcement surprised everyone. Damon almost spits out his water. Emily yelled, "That's great!" She jumped off of her chair and ran around to hug Carter. "I'd miss you, big brother." And his parents stared at Carter in bewilderment.

Emmitt asked softly and simply with concern, "Why?"

"Because of that," Carter pointed to Emily, "and because of all of you, because of the farm, my life. I don't think I can leave all of this." He spread his arms out and opened them up as if embracing them all.

His Dad stared at him and said, "Think about it more, Carter. Sleep on it. We'll talk about this tomorrow when we all digest what you're saying. What you're doing," Emmitt took a forkful of potatoes and shoved it into his mouth as if to say; we're done.

Carter didn't fold, "But, Dad, I know what I'm doing."

Emmitt finished chewing his food and said, "Carter, this is for mom and me to digest. This is a big decision. It is not something to decide at dinner."

Carter took a deep breath and murmured, "Yes, sir."

"And Carter," his Dad said.

"Yes!"

"Thank you for telling us. We know it wasn't easy for you."

"Thank you," Carter said. "I appreciate that."

"We'll all figure this out, son. Don't worry. Now, enjoy your meal. Tomorrow, we'll discuss this more thoroughly once we have weighed the pros and the cons."

"I vote that he stays," Emily grinned.

~ 34 ~

THE DECISION

After the family had breakfast, Emily gathered her books. Then, she ran toward the truck. Damon was going to drive her to school.

Emily then yells to her mom who is standing at the back door, "I vote that he stays."

"I heard you last night, honey," mom smiled. She then threw a kiss to them and turned to head back into the kitchen. Carter was by the sink cleaning the dishes. Emmitt was drying them. Sometimes, it's easier to do them by hand than placing them into the dishwasher.

When the last glass was cleaned and dried. Carter says, "Thanks for breakfast, mom."

"You're welcome."

"This is the stuff I'm going to miss. Simple things like breakfast with family, drying the dishes with Dad."

As if prompted by Carter's comment, Emmitt asks, "Do you all want to go into the living room and finish the dinner conversation from last night?"

They exited the kitchen. They all seated themselves in the living room; Emmitt and Rachel on the couch, Carter in a chair in front of them that he pulled over.

"OK, Carter. Tell us what you're thinking and how we can help you," his Dad said kindly.

Carter went through all the reasons why he wanted to stay. He had gone through the list, but Emmitt sat up when he got to his concern about his Dad's health. A rush of guilt and shame ran through Emmitt's body. Was he the reason for his son's change of mind? Sensing her husband's reaction, Rachel put her hand gently on his arm to settle him.

Rachel said, "It seems like you thought about this a lot, dear." This pause gave time for Emmitt to think about his health and what his son had said about it.

As his wife and son continued talking, Emmitt struggled with the guilt and shame rumbling through his mind. He was evaluating his selfishness, his self-regard. Then, finally, he realized that he was the wall obstructing everyone in his family from moving forward for what was best for them. It was as if a lightning bolt had charged through his body to shock him into cognizance.

Emmitt, lost in his thoughts; was oblivious to the talk in the room. The conversation between his son and his wife seemed like white noise. Emmitt then perked up and interrupted them, "Carter, you don't have to worry about me. I'm a much stronger man now. I am stronger because of you and the family. I get my strength from how you all challenge yourselves, how you strive for excellence in every way, and how you treat others with kindness, respect, and dignity.

Going to Boston College will expose you to so many unique, challenging, and insightful things. If you don't go, you will not grow. You will not become a better man. Dealing with leaving the family will make you stronger." His voice intensifies, "I'll be fine. The family will be fine. But, most of all, Carter, you'll be fine."

His Dad was right. He was absolutely right. "Dad, I hear you." He paused and looked thoughtfully at both of his parents. "Will you come to visit and see a game?"

"Yes, yes," Emmitt and Rachel said as they hugged each other.

"As long as we can have some lobstaw," Emmitt smiled.

Emmitt was the happiest Carter and his mother had seen him in a long time. Then, Carter was consumed with relief and with joy. Now, he felt good, real good, about his decision, but most of all, he was elated with his father's surge of optimism, hope, and wellbeing.

Carter yelled, "Go Eagles!!"

His parents jumped. Then Rachel in an uncharacteristic act thrust her fist into the air and whooped, "Go lobstaws!!"

Emmitt and Carter looked at her in shock. Carter said, "Mom, is that you?"

She meekly responds smiling, "Sorry. I got carried away."

The Good Man

PART II

"Good men are bound by conscience and liberated by accountability." - Wes Fesler

~ 35 ~

FLYING TO BOSTON

Carter sat nervously in waiting area of Gate 9 at the Detroit Metro Airport for his plane to be readied for flight. He had never travelled alone like this: huge airport, people rushing every which way, luggage being dragged. It was a mess.

Sure, he had been with the football team on flights, but that was different. He was surrounded by friends with commonalities which distracted him from any concerns. All the planning and logistics had been done for him. However, now, on this flight, he was on his own. He was nervous, confused; he was scared.

To make matters worse, his parents had driven from Kalamazoo to Detroit. The SUV, which they borrowed from the Rexes, was crammed with family and, of course, Charli. The conversation that filled the car on the way was of hope, excitement, football, and good stuff.

However, when he finally had to leave his family to catch his flight the emotions collapsed to the ground like a huge water balloon. His mom gave him a hug as her eyes became misty. That was tough. His brother gave him a big hug: a tight hug.

It gets worse. Emily started bawling. She hugged Carter and wouldn't let go.

Emmitt had to gently grab her and pull her away. "Come on, baby. He'll be back sooner than you know it." Little sis turned and wrapped her arms around her dad and buried her head into his chest sobbing.

Then Charli came up to Carter. Her face was flushed and tears trickled down her cheeks. "Carter, my best friend, I am going to miss you so much."

Carter couldn't stop the moisture from forming in his eyes. He draped his arms around Charli and whispered, "I'm going to miss you too, Charli." He stepped back, leaned forward and kissed her on the cheek.

Then tears flooded down her face. She hardly could get the words out. "Don't get weird on me, Carter." She then turned toward the SUV as did his family. They got into the car and looked out the window despondently at Carter and gave listless waves. Carter watched the car, his family, . . . his best friend as they drove away.

. . . .

Carter boarded the plane and took a window seat at the far back section. He didn't want to have to talk to anybody and was hoping that his choice of seats would leave him in isolation. Well, at least as much isolation as one can achieve on a plane.

He popped open his laptop and to search everything Boston and Boston College. He didn't want to get into Beantown blind. He hoped to have some knowledge of the topography, history, and culture as to be able to relate to his new surroundings and to the people.

He had gotten absorbed in his task. He was astonished by the history of Boston and its geography. He learned that Boston was once inhabited by the Shawmut Indian Tribe who lived along the Charles River. Boston was originally only a 789 acres peninsula that consisted of hills that the settlers later called Trimount: Mount Vernon, Beacon Hill and Pemberton Hill as well as hills named Copp's Hill and Fort Hill.

He was amazed to learn that these hills were dug up to fill in the bays around the city. The project began in the early 1800's and ended in the late 1880s. It more than doubled the landmass of the city.

He was so focused on his reading. He hardly heard the voice of a woman in the isle by his seat. "Well, look who it is?" Carter peeked up from his computer. The voice sounded familiar, but he looked bewildered. "Don't you remember me, Carter," the voice said sweetly.

Then it was like his brain came into focus. Yikes! It was Kathy. "I'm sorry. I didn't recognize you."

"I don't blame you. The last time you saw me I was a wreck."

He agreed. When he drove her home from his house back in the day, she looked like someone had thrown her into the drier. However, he thought to himself now: *She cleans up pretty good.*

"Is it all right if I sit here?" She pointed to the seat next to the isle.

"Of course," said Carter trying to mask his frustration in that not only someone was sitting in his row but that someone was Kathy.

"So, how have you been, Carter.? Why are you flying to Boston?" She paused for two seconds and continued, "I'm going home to visit my family." He nodded politely. "They live in Wellesley. Have you ever been in Wellesley, Carter?" He started to respond but she cut him off, "Oh, it is a beautiful town. Of course, there are a lot of beautiful towns in the Boston area." Carter smiled or was it more like a grimace as she rattled on, "There's Weston, Needham, and Dover which is a simply beautiful town with houses surrounded by woods and . . ."

"Excuse me, Kathy," interrupted Carter. "I don't mean to be rude, but I have to study up on Boston."

"Study up on Boston!? Why? I can tell you everything you want to know."

"Kathy, I'm going to Boston College and don't know hardly anything about the school nor the area."

"Boston College!? I didn't know that." She lied. She had seen on the news that Carter had elected to get his masters at Boston College and play football in Alumni Stadium, home of the Eagles.

"Kathy, yes. Now I have to study up. It's great seeing you." He turned and began to focus on his laptop leaving Kathy in an awkward, embarrassed state.

After about ten minutes, Kathy reached across the middle seat and gently touched Carter's wrist. He turned to look at her. Her eyes were watery. Her face was flushed. She whimpered, "Carter, I'm so sorry. I just . . . I just don't want to be known as that drunk girl." A tear meandered down her cheek.

Carter looked at her kindly. He shut his laptop and said, "Let's talk."

~ 36 ~

WELCOME TO BAWSTIN

Carter's extended chat with Kathy proved to be very revealing. Kathy hadn't had a drink since the infamous evening in the bar. She also had done extremely well at Western graduating early in the top of her class in business. Another revelation was that she had secured a position as a consultant at Bain & Company, a top five business in Boston. She certainly was far from being 'the drunk girl.'

Carter was proud of her and expressed that to her. She was going to live with her parents in Wellesley until she settled herself in Boston. When they exited the plane into Logan Airport, they said their good-byes. Kathy gave him a cordial hug and off she went. Carter watched her as she strolled away. *She really does cleanup really well.*

Carter headed for the baggage claim area with the cluster of travelers. As he stood on the escalator going down, he heard a man yelling, "Cawtaw. Cawtaw Dixon."

When Carter reached the bottom landing, he noticed the man holding a sign with his name on it. He was still yelling, "Cawtaw. Cawtaw Dixon."

Carter approached the short man and said, "Are you looking for Carter Dixon?"

"Yah, I am. What are ya, deaf?"

"I'm Carter."

"I'm Guido. Your driver. I'm goin' to take ya to Bawstin Cawlege. Get ya stuff and we'll blow this joint."

"This is all I have." Carter held up his carryon.

"That's it. Whadda ya wear the same stuff yeaw round."

"I travel light," Carter smiled.

On the way to the car, Guido looked up at Carter and said, "I thawt yous was supposed to be a fooball playa.?"

"I am, sir"

"How comes ya don't have big shouldaws and muscles awl ovaw da place?"

"Because I'm no big deal." He thought of his dad.

"We'll see abowt that when fooball season comes." I'll shows ya some of Bawston. I'll hook a uey hera."

As the wheels screeched, Carter said, "No. That's all right. We can just go to the school."

"Naw. We can't," Guido whined. He looked at Carter and smiled, "I gets paid by da owa."

So, the excursion was on. Carter found out that Guido worked part-time for B.C. driving. Boston College provided the vehicle. Guido painted full-time with his Irish buddy, Robert O'Malley.

They called themselves O.C. Painting. The O.C was for the odd couple.

"Why do you call yourselves the odd couple, sir?" asked Carter.

"Becaws, I'm Italiano and Bawby, I call him Bawby, becaws I'm his buddy. Oh yah, and becaws Bawby is Irish.

"OK," said Carter satisfied.

"Oh! And we're boat kindaw on the shawt side," said Guido. Then he glances at Carter, "By the way, call me Guido."

"Yes, sir"

Guido shakes his head and lets Carter's response float in the air thinking: *dis guy is dense.*

"Who thought of O.C. Painting?" Carter asks.

"I did," boasted Guido, sticking out his chest with a big grin. He was proud of his cleverness.

Guido gave Carter a historic tour of the city. He headed for downtown Boston, "Dars the Ole Nort Church, Cawtaw. Dats where da guys, Newman and Pulling, hung two lanterns to tell Americans dat da Brits were comin'. In 1775, da ole Nort Church was da tallest building in Boston. Not anymore," he laughed.

Then Guido drove to Tremont and Park Streets near the Park Street Church. "Where are we going now?" asked Carter.

"To da Granary Burial Ground. Dats wher Crispus Attucks is buried."

"Who's Crispus Attucks?" questioned Carter.

"Crispus Attucks was da first guy whos got killed in the Revolutionary War. Did yous knows dat he was a black guy?"

"No, sir" replied Carter, keenly aware now that he had a lot to learn.

"Well, he was," smiled Guido pleased with his knowledge. "Da first guy to die for our freedom was a black guy." He paused for a bit and then continued, ". . . John Hancocks, Paul Reveres and da parents of Ben Franklins is in dare too." Then he took a short turn and drove past the Boston Commons, the oldest park in the country. "Dat is where all dose ducklings is."

He went down the old combat zone which he told Carter had a bunch of strip joints back in the day. Then he took him to the North End, the Italian section of Boston and parked in the middle of the road outside of a place called Mike's Bakery.

"Wait here, Cawtaw. I's be right back." Guido jumped out of the car and waved to two guys on the sidewalk. They came out to the car and started directing traffic around the Nissan Murano. Carter watched the antics, the traffic and people with acute curiousity.

Guido popped out Mike's bakery holding a white paper bag. He looked at the two men, laughed, patted them on their backs and said a few things in Italian. "OK, Cawtaw. Here's da best cannoli in da world for ya."

The two men waved Guido out into traffic and gave him a thumbs up. He looked at Carter holding the bag. "Eat it, Cawtaw! It's not an onion."

Carter opened the bag and took a bite. His face said it all. It was the best in the world.

They drove down Storrow Drive along the Charles River. Sail boats glided along the glistening water with buildings in the background reaching up to the sky. The passed by Boston University which Guido said was not to be confused with Bawstin Cawlege.

They drove over a bridge into Cambridge. Guido pointed out Harvard and said, "dat's where all da smawrt people go. Not dat B.C. doesn't have a lot of smawrt people, but dat dare is as smawrt as they git: Hawvard and MIT."

They finally reached their destination: Ignacio Hall, Boston College. The ride was interesting and fun; Carter and Guido had connected. In fact, so much so that Guido asked for tickets to see Carter play while they were standing by the car.

"Hey, Cawtaw."

"Yes, sir."

Guido shook his head again, shook off Carter's 'sir' business and asked, "Cawtaw, can ya's get me some tickets for a game?"

"Sure. I think so. I'm not positive about the protoc..."

"Cawtaw, I'm just askin' for some tickets. Not your kidney."

Carter smiled, "Yes, sir." Guido shook his head yet, again. "How many would you like?"

"How about ten?"

"Ten???" I haven't even stepped onto the field, Guido."

Guido smiled at the fact that Carter finally called him by his name. "OK. Howa bout, four."

"I'll see what I can do."

"How will you contact me?"

"I have my ways," chuckled Guido. "See ya's!" He hopped into the car and drove off, leaving Carter in a strange place by himself with his carry-on, looking around like a lost puppy.

~ 37 ~

NOW, THAT'S ONE BIG GUY

Out of Ignacio Hall walks a huge black man. His smile stretched across campus, and his hand extended to Carter ten feet before he even got close. Carter reached out his hand. It disappeared into the man's massive grip. He could have crushed Carter's hand like a vice if he wanted to. The man didn't. He was gentle. Thank goodness, thought Carter.

"Hi! Are you Carter Dixon?" said the affable giant.

Carter already liked this place, this man. "Yes," Carter smiled back.

"Well, I'm Hal Krause, and I'm going to be your roommate during your graduate year at B.C." He reached down and grabbed Carter's carry-on.

"Come on. I'll get you settled in."

They walked into the dorm, which housed three hundred eighty-five students. It had a mixture of 4-person two-bedroom units and 6-person three-bedroom units. Hal opened the door to a second-floor unit that faced the inner campus.

"This is nice," said Carter looking around at the setting.

"It's a nice spot," said Hal. "It's relatively close to Alumni Hall and the Carroll School of Management, making it easy to get to practices and classes."

Hal asked if he'd like to see the campus. Though Carter was exhausted from the trip, he was excited to see Alumni Stadium, the home that Flutie built; that is the Doug Flutie who threw the *Miracle Pass* in the Orange Bowl to beat Miami.

Alumni Stadium was beautiful, with a seating capacity of 46,000. An average of 37,000 fans filled the stadium. Conte Forum, home to the Eagle hockey and basketball teams, is attached to the west grandstand, and the two facilities share a bank of luxury boxes.

Carter liked the idea of having the athletic facilities in close proximity. At Western Michigan University, Waldo Football Stadium, Read Field House, the home of Bronco basketball and volleyball, and Lawson Hockey Arena were relatively close but in separate parts of the campus. Though, he did like the fact that the facilities at Western had their own identity in location.

The campus was beautiful, with stone buildings reflecting the essence of the Catholic Church. Trees, flowers, and shrubs adorned the grounds, making it warm and welcoming.

When Carter got back to Ignacia Hall, he took a quick shower and flopped onto his bed. He had to get some sleep, for, in the morning, he had to meet with an academic counselor to set up his schedule and then onto football to meet the coaches and players.

Carter felt good about his decision, and he was snoring lightly before his head hit the pillow.

In the morning, Carter met with the coaches and the players. They later grouped them with position coaches. Next, the players received motivational talks and expectations about commitment to B.C. football and their behavior. Finally, coaches handed them a thick book of plays. That night they were to study and learn them quickly and thoroughly. One of the wide receivers scowled and glared at Carter for some no apparent reason. Carter felt uncomfortable but let it pass.

In the afternoon, Carter walked over to the Carroll School of Management to meet his tutor. When he got to the assigned room, he saw a massive black man. The guy must have been at least six foot eight inches tall and weighed roughly three hundred twenty pounds.

Carter walked up to him and said, "You must be waiting for the tutor?"

"Not exactly," he said as he flashed a broad white smile. "I am the tutor."

"Wow! You're a big guy."

"So, I've been told."

"I thought for sure you played football and were on scholarship."

"I am here on scholarship, but not for football: for engineering. I did my undergraduate work at UMass Amherst. Now I'm pursuing my masters."

"Well, I need a lot of help. You will earn your money when you tutor me. It might be harder than getting your masters. Hi, I'm Carter." He extended his hand toward the big fella.

"Nice to meet you, Carter. I'm Chris. Chris Greer."

~ 38 ~

HOLLISTON

Football had gone well. Carter had adapted to the schematics of the plays, and Hal and he would go over them each night even though Hal was a running back. A huge one at that.

At one of the first practices, it dawned on the players who Carter was. One of the safeties said, "Hey, aren't you the guy on that ESPN highlight video they keep showing?"

A linebacker looked at Carter and said, "Yeah, you sure are."

Carter felt awkward. A small crowd of players started to gather around him.

"What's going on here?" announced the wide receiver coach, Darrel Wyatt.

The players pointed to Carter. One of them said, "He is that guy on the ESPN highlight film. You know. Aw shucks."

Coach Wyatt certainly knew who Carter was. He had recruited him and said, "That was a great play, Carter."

"Aw Shucks. Thanks. Coach."

Head Coach Hafley overheard the chit-chat. "OK. Let's get back to work. You too, Shucks," he said, looking at Carter.

"Shucks. That works," said the big tight end, Bob Bicknell.

From then on, Carter became known as Shucks. He kinda liked it. The nickname reminded him of home.

He bonded with his new teammates. He found out that football is football wherever you play, that teammates are all family, and that coaches all want the same thing: to win.

However, that one wide receiver was a thorn in his side. When the other players kidded about calling Carter shucks, he leaned over to him and snarled, "Mucks. You know: shoveling horse crap. Carter found out that he was a junior named Antonio Cruz. He had performed very well on the field in his sophomore year.

He asked Hal about him, "Hal, what's the story with Cruz."

Hal said, "From what I've heard, Antonio is upset that you are here."

"Why?"

Hal looked at Carter incredulously and said, "Carter, you don't know?"

"No, Hal. I really don't know."

"Because you're a threat to his playing time. He was looking forward to a big year, and you come in and mix things up a bit."

"I don't mean to mess..."

"Carter. Cruz has got to grow up. He should know that football is about competition. Nothing is guaranteed." He paused, "... the same with life."

"But why would he call me Mucks?

"Because that's what people do when they want to tear others down, trying to build themselves up. They're immature. He has a lot of growing up to do, Carter."

"What should I do, Hal."

Hal looked at Carter and said, "Just be yourself, Carter. Just be Shucks."

The coaches gave the players two days off. Hal decided to take advantage of the free time and asked Carter if he would like to come to his hometown for a real meal. Not that the dorm food was bad. It was not bad at all. But his mom's cooking was the best.

Hal had a small Toyota Tacoma truck which was pretty old. It even had roll-down windows. And Hal was so big that he looked silly cramped behind the wheel. Carter wasn't going to tell him, though.

Hal chose to take Carter on the more scenic route. He drove down Rt. 135 to Newton Lower Falls. It was quaint and beautiful as the water rushed over the falls and under the bridge. They went through Wellesley, where Kathy, Robyn, and Joyce grew up. Kathy was right. It is a beautiful town.

They continue down Rt. 135 to the center of Natick. When they took a left onto Rt. 27, a band played in the Natick Common, and kids ran around playing. It reminded Carter of Paw Paw. When Hal told Carter that Natick was the home of Doug Flutie, Shucks nearly jumped out of his car.

They proceeded down Rt. 16 into Dover. Trees and historical farms mesmerized Carter. Then they got to a tree lined stretch of road bridged by overreaching branches. On the right was a wetland with two swans paddling around. Just beautiful.

When they were about to enter the town of Holliston, pointed to a small street and said, "That's where JoDee Messina grew up."

"You're kidding. Right? She is one of my dad's favorite country singers. Can we drive by and see her house?"

"Sure." Hal drove up to the intersection with an Italian restaurant, Bertuccis, on the left. He then banged a right as they say in Boston and then took another right onto Baker St. Hal then nodded his head in the direction of a gray A-frame colonial home. "That's it."

"If you don't mind, would you slow down so I can take a picture?" Hal nearly stopped, and Carter took the picture. Then, as they were driving to the end of the street, Carter texted a quick message to his Dad and sent the picture he had taken. "He won't believe this," said an elated Carter.

The tour continued. Hal drove to the small, picturesque downtown area. It reminded Carter of a Norman Rockwell scene with its New England architecture and quaint buildings.

"There's Fiskes Store, and that guy in the front is Mr. Paltrinari, a fixture in the town. On the right is the Holliston Superette. Great place for sandwiches. I'm going to bang a euy and drive past the high school."

When Hal and Carter passed the high school, they saw the football team practicing on Kamitian Field. "Hey, there's my old high school coach, Todd Kiley." Hal smiled, soaking in the memories. You could tell that he loved this town. And so did Carter. It was like Paw Paw in so many ways. He missed home.

The last place on tour was Hal's favorite: Out Post Farm. It was a turkey farm with a red barn from which they sold pies, vegetables, sandwiches of all varieties, and turkey. It was owned and run by Adrian Collins, a tall, humble, kind man whom Hal introduced to Carter. Hal grabbed a couple of sandwiches and a peach pie for his mom. All of this sure reminded Carter of home. Carter liked this town.

~ 39 ~

FOOTBALL AND FAMILY

Carter thought he wouldn't get much action being the new guy. However, B.C.'s first game was against Colgate. He ended up getting a lot of playing time as the score was 27 to 0 at halftime, during which he caught three passes from Junior Q.B., Phil Jurkovec. One was for a touchdown. By the end of the game, the score swelled to 51 to 0.

The early season had gone well. B.C. had won four in a row until Clemson tripped them up in a tight game at their place. They lost that one 13 to 19. Carter had become a household name among the fans. But, between his ESPN highlight and his new football heroics, Shucks remained humble.

He had texted his father earlier to see if he and the family could make it out to a game. They had decided on the North Carolina game since it was still warmer weather, and at B.C.

Carter was waiting for everyone in front of Alumni Stadium, where he stood next to the statue of Doug Flutie. The car pulled in, loaded with his family. All he could see were grins peeking out the windows. They poured out like a clown car. He ran up and hugged them all.

Dad had on his overalls. They made Carter smile. Rachel had her hair tied up and wore a light sweater over her blouse and a long blue skirt. Emily and Damon had on jeans and Western Michigan sweatshirts. Charli wore a white blouse and jeans. Her hair curled down to her shoulders. Strands partially covered her eyes. She looked elegant.

His father walked over to the statue, looked up at Flutie's pose throwing the football, reached up, and patted Flutie's foot. Emmitt looked back at us grinning.

"The Hail Mary. It seems just like yesterday," he beamed. But the reason he liked Flutie was not for his football. It was the father he was to his children and especially his son, Doug. His son has autism, and the miracle worker was hoping for more miracles. So, he did everything he could to raise awareness for autism. That's what Emmitt thought made Flutie a real hero.

"Look at this place," said Emily. "It's beautiful."

"Wow! Carter. I love the architecture of the buildings," said Charli.

Carter walked up next to her and put his arm around Charli, "So glad to see you. You look beautiful." She smiled back and hugged him. "Well, let me show you around while I have time."

They took the tour of campus and met people Carter knew. Charli noticed how nicely everyone dressed, even in casual clothes, and how confident they were. She looked down at her jeans and white blouse. She thought she was plain. Little did she know it, but her simplicity of dress was perfect.

When students passed by the group from Paw Paw, they greeted them with hello, and Carter was singled out with "Hey, Shucks." Others grinned when they looked at Emmitt's overalls. Emmitt smiled back, thinking that they sure were friendly here.

Charli noticed the coeds giving Carter more than a casual glance. She was so distracted that little did she notice the guys checking her out. But that was Charli.

~ 40 ~

OUCH!

Alumni Stadium was packed. Boston College had four wins and one loss up until this point. The fans were fired up for another victory, and the place was electric.

Antonio had been involved more and more in the offensive scheme, so his animosity toward Carter had waned. However, he would still shoot curious looks at Carter which made him uncomfortable. Both receivers were clicking on the field. Both had a lot to look forward to and wanted to make an impact. This game could be their signature performance.

The score was close after the first half—10 to 7 in favor of North Carolina State. After the catch, Carter had done well, hauling in three passes and dancing for extra yardage. But the second half was a different story for the team after N.C. State returned a fumble for a touchdown; the Eagles caved in, losing 7 to 33. Both Carter and Antonio had not played up to par and both felt the weight of the loss.

Carter's family hung over the railing where the players entered and exited the field. No one was happy: not the players, not the coaches, and not the fans. There was only one small group aside from N.C. State folks who were happy. That would be Carter and his family. Carter reached up and touched their hands.

"Sorry for the game," he said, holding his helmet.

They smiled down at him. Then, Emily piped in, "You were great, Carter. You caught some 'wicked awesome' passes. See! I'm getting this Boston lingo."

"Yes, you are, Emily. And thank you."

Damon said, "It was great seeing you out there, Bro."

"Bro?" quipped Carter.

"Well, I'm here in Boston. I'm trying to be cool."

"Well, be yourself, Bro," grinned Carter.

After dinner, the family hung out in Ignacio Hall and met Hal and some of Carter's other friends. When the uber came to pick everyone up, Carter was a little concerned about a replay of the Detroit airport scene. But, he was pleasantly surprised: there was none.

The family was warm and happy that they had had the opportunity to see him play, to see the campus, and to be able to hold him once more. However, Charli held on to him longer and a little tighter than expected. When she withdrew, Carter saw the water pooling in her eyes.

"You're my best friend. Carter."

"You're my best friend, Charli."

She slipped into the car. Then she was gone. His family was gone. He missed them already.

~ 41 ~

THE SQUEEZE

Carter was at the school of management with his tutor, Chris Greer. They had just gone over some statistic sheets, which were a challenge to Carter.

"How do you do this, Chris? It's all mumbo jumbo to me. This mean, medium, and mode stuff. Holy cow!"

Chris responds, "Carter, nothing is easy. I had to learn it just like you. After a while, I got the gist of it. Hang in there. It's all right to be frustrated, but don't quit, be patient, and it will come."

"Easy for you to say," Carter grinned.

"It wasn't easy when I was learning it, but now, yes. It is easy to say."

Time slid by, and the conversation somehow slipped from math to Chris when Carter posed a very poignant question to him without knowing how impactful it was.

Thinking of math, Carter asked, "Chris, what was the most monumental problem you ever faced?"

Chris thought for a moment as his face sagged with uneasiness. Then, finally, he looked Carter straight in the eyes and said, "Racism."

Carter backed up a little in his chair. He was expecting something along the lines of calculus or numerical analysis, but not that.

"Racism?" Carter said gently. "How's that, Chris?"

"Everything I've ever done or achieved was challenged because I was black," said Chris with a heavy voice. "Fortunately, my parents prepared me to a certain extent for the name-calling and even the resistance from other schools when I competed in a math competition. I was greeted with, 'Oh, he can't do that well. He's black.' Something along those lines"

Carter had a complex time understanding. He had never confronted any racism because he is white and lived in a predominantly white world.

"But you were able to shake it off?"

"Every day, Carter, when I walk down the street, some people will take a few steps to the side, or I will get a look . . ."

"What kind of a look?"

"A look like I might be a threat to them. And you know, Carter. I don't really blame them. Every time I watch the news and see a black face committing a crime, I can't help but get pissed off at the offender."

"But that's not you, Chris. It shouldn't affect you?"

Chris leans his massive body forward in his chair and murmurs, "Carter, it affects me and every black man and woman everywhere."

"But how? You're a great guy. You're intelligent. You're . . . "

Chris interrupts him, "Carter, I'm black. Every time a black man is on the news for something terrible, it feeds into the stereotype of blacks being stupid and criminals." His voice raises a couple of notches, "They, those blacks, are the actual racists against all blacks. They erase the sacrifices and accomplishments of all those folks who have benefited society.

Dr. Charles Drew, a black man, designed a procedure to preserve blood so it could be stored for transfusions. Because of him, millions of lives have been and are saved throughout the world. Patricia Bath, a black woman, invented a tool and technique to remove cataracts using a laser beam called the Cataract Laserphaco Probe. Otis Boykin developed the control unit for pacemakers. Valerie Thomas invented the Illusion Transmitter that greatly enhanced NASA research." Carter sat in amazement and had no idea about these black folks or their contributions.

Chris finished venting his frustration, "Blacks invented the golf tee, the imaging x-ray spectrum, air conditioning, the fire extinguisher, the lawnmower, the typewriter, the home security system, and more. Yet, the only thing people remember is these jerks who commit crimes and taint black lives."

Chris let out a breath of air. "I don't blame you," said Carter. "For you being upset. I'm sorry. I . . ."

A knock at the door grabs their attention. It opens slowly, and a short man with jet black hair peeks into the room. Then he saunters up to Chris and says, "Wow, you sure is a big football playa."

"I'm not the football player," Chris said. Then he turns to Carter, "He is."

"Sorry bout dat."

"No problem. I get that all the time."

"Cans I talk toos dat football playa alone?"

Chris turns to Carter, "I guess we're finished, Carter. I'll go collect my items in the next room, so you guys can talk."

Carter then asks the gentleman, "What's up, sir?"

"'Sir'. . . I like dat," he muses. "Well, Cawtaw. We heard yous fader needs some cash. Somethin' bout a mad cow."

"What? I never heard anything like that from my Dad. So how did you find out?"

"Wees have our ways, Mr. Cawta. Dat don't matta. What does matta is dat wese gots some monies for yas to helps out."

"Who's we and why would you give me money?"

"The wees don't matta. The monies, however, does." Carter listens. He's suspicious and confused, and concerned.

"Cawtaw, all yous gots to do is drop a pass or two next game."

"I can't do that," Carter blurted. "I won't do that!"

"Yeahs, ya will." The man drops a role of hundred-dollar bills on the table. "Dares five-thousand bucks," Cawtaw. "Now ya's a playa." He turns abruptly, bolts out of the door, and slams it shut.

Chris enters from the other room. "Don't do it, Carter. You'll never play football again."

~ 42 ~

MOLLY O'MALLEY

In nice, dry weather, Molly O'Malley would roll her bike onto the trolley in Boston's South End where she lived. Then, when she arrived at the Brighton stop on Commonwealth Ave., she would pull her bike out and ride it to Boston College.

Today, Molly rode her worn, blue Schwinn bicycle to Ignacio Hall. Her vibrant, deep red hair flowed behind her. A broad smile radiated from her face.

She settled her bike gently on the ground by the back door leading to the dorm kitchen. She strolled into the culinary area and was greeted kindly by fellow employees.

"Hi, Molly," said a sweet, plump black woman. "I'm ready to go."

"You're not going anywhere, Mona. We've got work to do," laughed Molly.

"We sure do," said a taller black girl as she handed Molly the hair net.

"Thanks, Cheryl."

"Hey, what's happening, girl?" a voice from the stove area called out.

"Not much, Kyle with Style," she yelled back.

Molly loved this kitchen crew. The three of them road the trolley to B.C. from Roxbury. On occasions, Molly would catch the same trolley, and they would engage work talk among other things. Mona and Cheryl became particularly close to Molly and would do anything for her. Molly loved them all. They were diversified, hard-working, and fun. To her, it was the dream job working with such good people.

....

In the morning, Carter had called his Dad to ask him if everything was OK. His father said they had some financial problems, but Larry Lueth, an officer at the First National Bank of Michigan in Kalamazoo, was helping him navigate the situation. Emmitt had no idea what Carter was talking about when it came to mad cow disease, but he did say root rot from too much rain caused a shortage in crops. So, when Carter mentioned the money to throw the game, his father was shocked.

"You do anything like that, Carter. You will never be welcome back to the farm again." Carter held out his cell phone and looked at it like he was looking at his father. "But, Carter, I know you will do the right thing."

"Don't worry, Dad. I will. Oh, Dad. I have a very important question."

Emmitt wasn't exactly prepared for another shocker. He delicately replied, "What's that, son?"

"How's Oatmeal doing?"

....

Before lunch, Carter had shared the conversation between Chris and himself with Hal, his roommate. Hal echoed everything Chris had said about being black. But he carried it one step further.

"Carter, you know how Chris said that every time a black person appears on TV for committing a crime, it paints all blacks as criminals to racists."

"Yeah. I never thought of it before, but I understand what Chris was saying," said Carter.

"I have a question for you, Shucks."

"What's that?"

"When a white guy robs a store, commits a shooting or even worse, do you think that all whites are criminals?"

Carter pondered the question and eventually responded, "No! I don't, Hal. You make a good point. How can people get rid of racism?"

"Racism will always exist. Folks like to use it as a way to feel that they are better than others. All you, I and others can do is be kind and respectful to others; to set an example."

"That's not always easy to do, Hal."

"It's not." Then a wide smile stretched across Hal's brown face as he said, "Chose love over hate. It is the right thing to do."

"Now you sound like my father."

Hal also addressed the bribe to Carter to have him miss a pass and throw the game. He told Carter that he would never see him again if he took the money. Carter told him it was never a thought. His father's words again rang in his head: *Do the right thing.*

Carter was shaken by how emphatic Hal expressed himself about taking any money. But Carter was also impressed with

Hal's honesty, his integrity. Shucks was *more* than glad to have a friend like Hal: he was honored.

Hal and Carter made their way to the cafeteria around noon.

Molly was serving at the buffet area. Carter had seen her often: enchanted with her freckles, brown eyes, and vibrant red hair which peek-a-booed from under her hairnet.

Her smile lit up the room as she asked Carter, "What would you like?"

He read her name tag, put on the charm, and responded, "Hi, Molly, I'll have some chicken and a large spoonful of mashed potatoes."

"Yes, Mr. Carter," Molly said with disinterest.

"How do you know my name?" asked Carter.

"I read your name tag." He looks down for the nonexistent tag. Then she turns to put some dishes in place.

"My name tag?"

"I'm just messin' with you, Carter. Everybody knows you on campus. You're a big deal on the football team."

"I'm not a big . . ."

"Save it, Carter. I don't date football players at B.C. Or for that matter, hockey players, basketball players, baseball . . . you get the point." She faces him with her hands on her hips. "Too many of them think that they're big shots. That . . ."

"I'm not like that."

"Sure, Carter. And my hair is not red." She looks at the students in line, "Next!" End of conversation. Carter knew he would see her again at the Ignacio commissary. But he wanted more than a brief chat. He wanted to meet this girl, to know this girl, . . . to date this girl. A real date would be a first for him.

~ 43 ~

JULIE VISITS

Julie was in Boston for a convention at Harvard on in-depth research techniques. However, she made sure that she set aside a chunk of time to see Carter and check in on his progress, his life, and a little more.

She is excited to see him. Julie has a soft spot in her heart for her goofy former student. So she drove up to the front of Ignacio hall with anticipation. Even though it was relatively early, the moon hung in the sky and pushed a gentle light through the cold fall air.

Carter was waiting outside and waved like a little kid when he saw her arrive. Carter wore a blue sports jacket, a V-neck sweater, and Kaki pants. He slid into the passenger side of the rental, a modest gray Kia, and gave Julie a quick hug.

"Thanks, Carter. I missed you, too," she said. She glanced at him. "Wow, Carter. Look at that outfit. You've really become gentrified since coming out east."

"Is that good? I mean, gentrified. It sounds good."

"Yes, it's good, Carter," Julie grinned. "You're still the same old Carter. Thank goodness."

They took a booth in the back of the restaurant away from students and customers. Julie didn't want to compete with clients' chatter while talking.

They ordered a vegetable pizza and two glasses of water. As they waited for their meal, Carter talked about how he enjoyed Boston and B.C. but still missed home. When the pizza arrived, Julie took over the conversation.

"So, Carter. How's school going?"

"Good. Real good. I have a tutor who helps me out, but he's not as cute as you."

"Carter put a lid on it." She smiled. "In many ways, you haven't changed, Carter.

"Is that good or bad?"

"A little bit of both, Carter. But I have to admit; I'm very proud of you. You got your undergraduate degree from Western, and now you're getting your masters from Boston College. Not many people can say that they've gotten their masters."

Carter's face blushes with humble embarrassment. "I appreciate that, Julie. But, hey, would you like to go to a football game? We have one tomorrow against Florida State.

"Well, I appreciate that, but I don't like football."

"I didn't know that." Carter was surprised. "But you came to a game at Western?"

"I came to give you support. That was it."

"Why don't you like football?"

"Carter, I don't like many sports. When my brother got hurt in the accident, he was forever confined to a wheelchair. It hurts me too . . ."

"But didn't he go to sporting events? I thought you mentioned that he went to a Preds hockey game in Nashville."

"He did and does. I went with him. We parked his wheelchair in the space for the disabled. He loved the fans, the bands, and the entire event. It wasn't just a hockey game. He would watch the players fly around the ice." Her face dropped a bit.

"And...?"

"And he was excited watching them. Too excited. People around were screaming, jumping up and down in their seats, kids were running to get food, and he," She hesitated. "... and he was limited to only watching.

I looked at him and knew that in his mind, he wished that he could be skating, running, jumping out of his seat. He had accepted his fate. But, selfishly, foolishly, I didn't. I bear the pain of his limitations.

"Wow! I'm so sorry," Carter offered in attempted support.

She brushed the comment aside and took a deep breath, "Carter, that's life. I've got to learn better to deal with it and move on." Then, changing the subject totally and abruptly, she says, "By the way, Carter. I forgot how good-looking you are."

"Aw, shucks. And you look beautiful, Julie. You really do." Even though she was a few years older than Carter, he was attracted to her. He liked her combination of intelligence, spunkiness, and being pretty in a business way.

They chatted for a few more minutes. Then Julie had to leave for an appointment. When they got up to say goodbye, Julie leaned over, hugged Carter, and kissed him on the cheek.

"Thank you," he said. Then Julie slapped him on the side of the face. "What's that for?" He put the palm of his hand to his cheek which now was pink.

"I just want you prepared for the unexpected in life, Carter." She turned to walk out, stopped, and faced him again. She reached up to pull back a lock of hair that had fallen over her eyes. He flinched and lifted his hands to shield his face. She smiled, "Don't worry, I'm not going to hit you again." A slight pause. "I love you, Carter." Then she walked toward the door, waved goodbye over her shoulder, and drifted away.

Still holding the palm of his hand on his stinging cheek, Carter stared as she vanished into the darkness. "I love you, too," he whispered.

On Saturday, Boston College played their game against Florida State. Unfortunately, they lost a squeaker, 23 to 26. More unfortunately, Carter missed a pass in the end zone in the last minute, which would have won the game for B.C.

~ 44 ~

TICKETS

The following Tuesday evening, Carter was seated with Chris, his Boston College tutor, deciphering some stubborn calculous problems. They were making some headway when there was a knocking on the door. The Cigar Guy, who twisted Carter's arm to throw a game, entered without being invited in. He had a big smile plastered across his face and carried a big wad of bills.

Hal rises from his seat, looking like a massive tree that had suddenly grown. "I'll wait in the other room."

Carter stands as well. "I'd appreciate it if you could stay here, Hal"

"Carter, I don't want anything to do with this, and I . . ."

"Please, Hal. Just wait!"

Hal sat down disconcerted. "I'll do it for you, Carter. But if it gets dicey, I'm outta here."

The Cigar Guy then says, "Maybe we can gives yas a cut of the action." Hal glares back at him. If looks could kill, that guy would be dead.

The guy smiles at Carter, "Yous done good, Cawtaw. Now dares more mulla for yas." He extends his hand holding a clump of bills, and waves it in front of Carter's face.

Carter reaches into his pocket and pulls out the original stack of hundred-dollar bills he had gotten from the man. "I'm not taking it. And here's the money you gave me," he snaps." Carter pushes the money toward Cigar Guy's face. "I didn't miss that catch on purpose. It was out of my reach. Believe me. If I could have caught it, I would have pulled it in and held it tight like a newborn baby."

"It don'ts mattaw, Cawtaw. Yous din't catch it. Ya's done good, and dares..."

The door flies open pushing Cigar Guy behind it. "Hey, Cawtaw. Where's my tickets?" Guido quacks in a cheery voice.

Cigar Guy pushes the door away, exposing himself to Guido for the first time. "What you's doin' here, Guido?"

"The bigger question is 'what you's doin' here', Vinny?" Guido responds.

Chris stared at the scene like it was a segment from *The Godfather*.

"Hey!!! Wait a minute. Ya's tryin' to squeeze my boy, Cawtaw?" He glances at Carter and then back to the man.

"Ah, no. Wells, I guess so."

Guido sees the money in Vinny's hand. Then he sees the money in Carter's grip. "Let's clean this up now. Vinny, yous put dat money back in you's pocket." Then he looks at Carter. "What's dat money for?"

Carter says, "It was what he gave me before the last..."

Guido halls off and slaps Carter across the face knocking him back onto the table where Chris was sitting watching the chaos unfold. "Yous jerk, Cawtaw. Give Vinny the mulla back," he snarls.

Carter makes his way carefully around Guido and hands Vinny the money. "Here," he says quietly.

"Tanks," replies Vinny sheepishly.

Guido then walks up to Vinny and slaps him much harder than he did Carter. Vinny falls back against the door and almost falls to his knees.

"Get the hell outta here, Vinny."

"What am I goin' to tell the boss?" he quivers.

"Tell him, 'Guido says that Cawtaw is off limits. Now get outta here before I . . ." Vinny slithers out of the doorway and scrambles down the hall. Guido turns to Carter, smiles, and calmly says as if the entire incident never happened, "Where's my four tickets, Cawtaw?"

~ 45 ~

TROUNCED

It was a sunny but cold day in Chestnut Hill, the site of Alumni Stadium. The Eagles were facing a tough, ten-win, one-loss Wake Forest team. This game was B.C.'s last chance to salvage what had been a disappointing season. Expectations were high initially but had dropped like a boulder from the sky after the Florida State game.

Only about 25,000 fans turned out for the game in a stadium that could seat over 44,000.

As Carter was warming up for the game, an errant ball nestled up against the sidelines. He went to retrieve it, and he heard yelling.

"Cawtaw. Cawtaw!"

Carter looked up, holding the retrieved football, and there was Guido with and gentle-looking man. Carter then said, "Hi Guido. Unfortunately, I don't have time to . . ."

"Yah, yous do. This here is my buddy, Bawby." Then he turned and pointed up to the stands. "And dares Bawby's wife and little girl."

Carter looked up with the sun glaring in his eyes. All he could see were a flock of fans. Carter waved to the blur. Then he looked at Bobby and said, "Nice to meet you, sir. I hope we bring you a win." He then turned, ran off, and yelled back, "I've got to go!"

"Yous betta win, Cawtaw. Wees don'ts wants to stand in da colds for nuttin," screamed Guido.

Well, they didn't win. They got trounced by Wake Forest. At half-time, the score was twenty-four to ten in favor of Wake. There was still some hope. The stands had thinned out except for the hard core, optimistic fans. However, they even groaned in disappointment as the Deacons shut out the Eagles in the second half to make the final score forty-one to ten.

The only touchdown had been a pass reception by Antonio Cruz from Jurkovec in the first half.

When the game ended and the team disappeared into the tunnel under Conte Forum to their lockers, three girls yelled down to Carter. He was still on the field and had not yet left. It was his last game at Alumni Stadium. He wanted to soak it all in even with the loss.

"Hey, Carter," the three girls screamed in unison, waving their arms wildly in the air, trying to get his attention. Carter stopped just short of exiting the field and looked up. There were Kathy, Robyn, and Joyce: the three amigas.

Kathy yells down, "We'll meet you out at the entrance of Conte Forum." It was like they had coordinated the get-together with him. They had not. Carter was surprised to see them.

Guido then yells down, just before Carter entered the tunnel, "Hey Cawtaw. Yous gots me losin' tickets. I wants my monies back." He laughs, "I's jus kiddin'. Sorry, yous lost and tanks for the tics." He follows that up with, "Yous mus be a babes magnet. I saw dems girlies."

. . . .

After the final talks by the coaches about the game and season, Carter met the girls at the front entrance to Conte Forum. They exchanged niceties when Kathy asked Carter if they could treat him to dinner. The next thing he knows, he's sitting in a booth next to Kathy with Joyce and Robyn sitting across from them at the Red Lobster Restaurant.

"This is a great restaurant," says Joyce.

"Yes, it is. You'll love the lobstaw," adds Robyn.

Kathy just smiles. She's in heaven sitting next to her dream.

When Carter attempts to eat his lobster, the girls laugh at his struggles to pry the meat out from the claws. Even funnier is the grimace on his face. Some of the fluids leak out of the tail."

"This is gross! Yuck! You girls really like this stuff?"

"Yes. We do." They replied between giggles.

Once Carter could secure a small clump of meat and dip it into the butter, he liked it too. "Hey, this is pretty good." He thought about his family. He still owed them a lobster dinner.

During the meal, Kathy stopped feeding herself and looked at Carter. Then, she said bluntly, "Are you interested in me, Carter?"

Joyce and Robyn almost choked on their fish. Finally, Joyce asks, "Kathy, what kind of a question is that?"

"It's an honest question."

"This is probably not the time or place for such a private . . . question," inserts Robyn.

"I don't care about the time or place. I care about the answer," Kathy proclaims. She turns to face him and crosses her arms. "Well, Carter. What is the answer?"

Carter thought to himself; *this is awkward. How do I deal with this?* He didn't want to hurt her feelings, and he sure didn't know she felt so strongly about him. His eyes searched the restaurant as if the answers were in the air.

Finally, Carter says, "Kathy, you're a great girl."

"Does that mean you're interested in me?"

"What do you mean by 'interested?'" He was still searching. He needed time to figure this out.

"I mean, would you like to be my, my . . ." Robyn and Joyce leaned forward. They didn't want to miss this. Kathy continued, "Let me be candid. Would you ever want to marry me? There I said it." She let out a gasp of air, releasing the tension within her.

Carter sat baffled. This was not the type of dinner conversation he had expected. He had to try to control the situation. He reached over to Kathy, put his arm around her, and said, "Kathy, I am too young, too confused, especially now, to answer such a monumental question."

"To what monumental question? 'Are you interested in me?'" she sobs.

"Kathy, you essentially asked if I would marry you."

"Well?"

"Kathy, you are my friend. As are all of the people I meet. I am sorry if I gave you any false impressions, false hope."

Kathy dropped her head onto his shoulder. "I am too."

Joyce and Robyn soaked in the tender moment with sadness and a tremendous sense of relief.

~ 46 ~

FATHER ADORNO

Hal and Carter had gone to the cafeteria to catch a snack. Molly was serving, but Carter didn't coerce any extended conversation. He gave his order. A smile and thank you completed the task. Molly smiled back and then attended to the next student. Carter was hoping for more. However, that door had shut on him.

Surprisingly, many of the tables were occupied. The students were gearing up for finals. A break was always necessary.

While Hal and Carter talked, Carter noticed two guys and a priest engaged in conversation and laughter. They seemed to be enjoying each other and the conversation. Hal and Carter had finished their snack. Carter said he would take the plates away, and Hal would meet him back in the room. As Carter was leaving, he noticed that the two students had gone. The priest stayed behind to finish up his sandwich.

Carter decided that this would be a good time to talk to a priest. After all, he had been on campus for a few months at a Catholic school and felt obligated to know more about Catholicism.

He approached the priest and said, "Hi, sir. Mind if I sit with you for a bit?"

"Not at all, son."

"Thank you. I'm Carter Dixon." He extended his hand.

The father shook it and said, "I'm father Adorno, and I know who you are." Carter noticed the priest's partially bandaged hand, and the exposed layers were red and crinkled.

"How do you know me?" asked Carter.

"I try to attend as many sporting events as possible here at B.C. I love to see the kids engaged and representing their school. I've seen you on the football field catching passes and evading tacklers. It's an honor to meet you, Carter," he smiled. "Now. What's on your mind?"

Carter hadn't prepared for this meeting and didn't know what he wanted to say. He just knew he wanted to interact with this man. So he began with the obvious, "What happened to your hand?"

Father Adorno lifts his hand and looks at it. "It's a long story."

"I've got time, Father. As long as you do."

"Well, Carter. I wasn't always a priest." Carter listened respectfully. "I was a fireman. One day we got a call for a blaze in a four-story dwelling on Beacon Street. We had three trucks and an ambulance respond.

The hoses were blasting through a second-story window with flames clawing out. There were people inside the building screaming. My buddy, Ross, and I ran in and clomped up the stairs, boots and all, to try to reach them." He looks down, recalling the incident.

Carter remained silent letting the priest continue. "We managed to break through the door. My fire buddy, Ross, reached for a young girl whose clothes were in flames. Davey, another fireman, came in from behind me to help. But, unfortunately, as he was trying to pull a little kid to safety, he fell through the floor."

Carter could tell that this was not easy for Father Adorno. "Oh, my gosh!" he uttered, regretting asking about the father's hand.

"I reached out to grab him, but he disappeared below. I took my fire jacket off and wrapped it around the kid, smothering the flames. I started to burn up like cardboard. Someone pulled the boy from me, and I can't remember anything after that. "

"That's terrible," responded Carter, horrified.

"I found out later that Davey had died. Ross had made it with a few burns, and firefighters had rescued five people. I ended up at Peter Bent Brigham Hospital, where Dr. Nierenberg and Dr. Twarog saved me. Carter, those two doctors, and the nurses stayed with me for two months until I fully recovered. I have God to thank for them and my life. So I am returning the favor to God."

"Do you ever see the doctors?" asked Carter.

"All the time. They're the best. On occasions, I go to Dr. Nierenberg's temple and throw the bull around with the Rabbi and the doctor's Jewish buddies. Sometimes, Dr. Twarog will join us. But usually the three of us will meet for dinner someplace."

"It's nice that you all get together," said Carter. He was relieved that the story was easing from tragic to bearable. "I'm so sorry about you losing your friend, Father."

"So am I, Carter. I am despondent because I never told Ross that I loved him." The Father looked at Carter and smiled, "Always tell people that you love them. Let them know that they are valued."

Carter responds, "My father preaches the same type of thing."

"That's good. Your father is a good man. But, unfortunately, I see too many people whose parents or loved ones leave this world, and those left behind carry the burden of guilt and shame."

"Guilt and shame?"

"Yes, Carter. Their last words to them may have been 'I hate you' or 'I don't love you,' because they weren't grateful for something or someone. It's sad."

Carter made a mental note to himself to always treat others with love. Carter and Father became good friends. Father laughed when Carter told him he had gone to mass one time and that it was more challenging than football practice: stand up, sit down, kneel, stand up again, kneel.

Carter didn't understand the mass with so much spoken in Latin, but he liked the sermons. For example, "Love thy neighbor."

~ 47 ~

THE LIBRARY

Carter needed some research for a project in one of his business classes. He tried to procure the information online but was unsuccessful. Carter had to go to the library. It was like going to a foreign country for him, but he had no choice.

As Carter walked to the library, light snow fell from the clouds, and a chill rippled through his body. However, he liked the cold, the snow, and the winter. It reminded him of home and his family.

Lost in thought, he didn't notice the man running across the campus toward him.

"Carter! Carter! Wait a minute." Carter looked at the man heading toward him. He recognized him even without a football uniform. It was Antonio Cruz. Carter didn't know if he should take a protective stance or remain standing for a second. He decided to stay put but with caution.

"Shucks, thanks for waiting," Antonio said, panting.

Carter liked it that he didn't call him Smucks. That was quite an improvement from their previous interactions.

"No problem, Antonio. What's up?"

"Hey, Carter," Antonio said, still gasping for air, "I just want to say I'm sorry for being a jerk."

"Wow, Antonio. I appreciate that. You were a little nasty there."

"I know. I had to grow up. Football is competition. I'll be a better player next year because of you."

"Actually, Antonio, you'll be a better player because of yourself. It takes a strong man to look inward for faults and correct them. Willing to admit you were wrong is not an easy thing to do. Thank you."

"So, Carter. When you graduate, let's keep in touch, Bro."

Carter smiled. He had gone from Smuck to Shucks to Carter to Bro. He said to Antonio, "That would be great. I'll be following your game next year, Bro."

They gave each other a quick man hug and exchanged their 'Later, Bros.' They headed in opposite directions. Carter started for the library and Antonia to who knows where.

The Thomas P. O'Neill, Jr. Library was located conveniently near the center of campus. Carter walked in, went directly to the reception desk, and smiled, "I need help."

"What kind of help?" smiled the young co-ed. "Would you like to have me connect you with a personal instructor or . . ."

"A personal instructor would be great. Thank you."

Carter waits momentarily as the receptionist makes a phone call. She eventually turns to Carter, "You're lucky. There is a student helper available. Usually, you have to make an appointment."

"Great," replies Carter.

"Take the elevator," she points in the direction, "to the fifth floor. Your work area will be room 512."

Carter thanks her and proceeds to the fifth floor, room 512.

Room 512 seemed to be elusive to Carter. However, he found it once he got his bearings and read the directional board. Carter knocked gently on the door.

"Come in," said a sweet voice.

Carter pushes the door open and steps in. "What are you doing here, Molly? He says in surprise.

"I'm reorganizing books," she says in a flat tone. He had not seen her without a hair net. To Carter, she looked beautiful.

Molly had pulled her glistening dark red hair up in a ponytail. She was wearing a dark grey V-neck with a pinkish blouse playfully peeking out from the top. She had dark jeans on and hiking boots.

"What are you doing here, Carter? I didn't think you even knew where the library was."

"I need help."

"I'll say you do," Molly kidded.

"Do you work here?" asked Carter, confused.

"I'm studying, and I work here?"

"Do you go to B.C.?"

"No! I go to B.U," Molly snaps back sarcastically. "Carter, you've got to stop asking questions. You're getting dumber by the minute.

Embarrassed, Carter replies, "I'm sorry. I didn't know you went to school here."

Molly lets a breath of air out. "I'm sorry, too, Carter. I should not have been so snippy. Have a seat." She gestures with her hand to a chair situated beside her.

Carter sat down next to Molly. They chatted a little before diving into the studies. It turned out that she attended B.C.'s school of nursing at night and worked as a personal assistant at the library and in the kitchen at Ignacio Hall. The college supplemented her classes because she was an employee at B.C.

Molly also commuted from home to save money. Carter was impressed that she brought her bike onto the transit car and then rode it from the station to B.C. when the weather permitted. She was intelligent, a worker, diligent, and self-sufficient. Carter liked all of that. Plus, she was spunky.

Molly guided Carter through the research process. She was a good teacher and very professional; Julie-type in her business demeanor. They both enjoyed the study session. When it ended, Molly surprised Carter.

"Have you ever been to George's Island in the Harbor," Carter?

"No! I haven't."

"Well, let's go later in the month. It won't be as cold then. You'll love it."

Carter doesn't hesitate and says, "That would be great. How do I . . ."

Molly gets up from her chair and heads for the door. She opens it and turns to face Carter. "Don't worry, Carter. I'll give you the date, the time, and the information you need."

"How will I get there?"

"You'll figure it out, Carter," she smiles and closes the door.

Carter sits back in his chair, clasps his hands behind his head, and smiles, a genuine big smile. "My first real date."

~ 48 ~

THE FERRY

Good thing Molly waited for the weather to improve. It had been cold and damp until today. She lucked out in booking the tickets for the sun peeked behind a few clouds and warmed the air. None-the-less, sweaters and jackets were necessary: if not for the island, certainly for the boat.

Molly waited by the entrance to the New England Aquarium watching the seals pop up from their confined pool. It was about 9:15 a.m. Carter was to be there at that time. Their cruise boat was to leave at about 10:00.

Three yellow buses with Natick Schools labeled on their sides pulled up. Teachers hopped out and then the students streamed off chatting with excitement.

These educators were professionals and had everything under control. Molly watched with curiosity and amazement on how the teachers lined up the students into groups of five behind either chaperones or a teacher. The kids all had on red t-shirts with Wilson Middle School across them. However, it was difficult to read the lettering because of the jackets the students were wearing.

The kids were calling out the teachers' name when confused. "Where should I go, Mrs. McClain" or "Who is my chaperone, Ms. Mehal." A tall educator with a grin like Johnny Carson and a Notre Dame baseball hat directed students. Molly was entranced with the logistical choreography coalescing before her eyes.

Molly almost forget about Carter when all of a sudden, he comes squeezing through several lines of youngsters. At first, Molly thought he was one of the chaperones until he began waving at her and grinning like one of those middle school kids. Molly thought that he could have been one of them, but he towered over the kiddos.

"Hi, Molly!" he grinned excitedly. "We're going to the Aquarium, too?"

"No such luck, Carter. We're going to board that boat over there." She pointed to a large ferry docked at Long Wharf.

"Awesome."

"It won't be awesome if we miss boarding," she said. She grabbed Carter's hand and pulled him in the direction of the ramp leading to the boat. "Here's your ticket, Carter. Don't' lose it."

"You've got to have more faith in me than that, Molly," he said, lightly squeezing her hand.

She looked up smiling and rolled her eyes. "I'll try, Carter."

The Ferry ride to the island was a little chaotic. The buses full of students weren't going to the Aquarium. They were going to Georges Island, and they were passengers along with Molly and Carter. Not that they were bad. They weren't. However, they were kids running around the boat, talking loud, and just having fun.

Molly and Carter didn't mind. It was interesting watching the antics of the students and how the teachers monitored them.

"I wonder if I had that much energy when I was their age?" asked Molly.

"I hope so," Carter nodded his head to the kids, "That's what being young is all about." It was obvious that he was enjoying the scene unfolding in front of them.

~ 49 ~

GEORGES ISLAND

When they got to the thirty-nine acre island, the Natick crowd had dispersed onto the grounds with their groups like they were shot out of a canon. Carter and Molly looked at each other with relief. It now was relatively quiet except for the distant voices of the groups.

Molly and Carter walked the grounds. They both were intrigued with the information written on markers of this National Historic Landmark. Although, Molly had been there several other times, she always learned something new.

Originally, the island was used for agriculture for two hundred years. In 1825, the U.S. government procured the island for coastal defense. Over the next twenty years, Fort Warren was built from granite mined in Quincy, Massachusetts. In 1847, the fort was completed and became one of the country's finest coastal defensive structures. Because of the design, tucked in between two drumlins of land, the ramparts were hardly visible from the harbor.

However, the fort never was needed to defend the harbor. It was used for a training ground, a patrol point, and a Civil

War prison. It was decommissioned in 1947 and acquired by the Massachusetts Department of Conservation.

Carter and Molly toured the walkways, guardhouse, mess hall, the gun batteries, and the various buildings that were embedded in the topography as well as several free-standing buildings located in training grounds at the center of the fort.

By now, they had removed their sweaters as it became hotter. Carter and Molly were exhausted and rested on the rocks adjacent to the small beach area.

"This place is amazing," said Carter. "It was cool reading about how well the Civil War prisoners were treated, and that 'The Battle Hymn of the Republic' originated here."

Molly remained quiet and gazed out at the city skyline. Wispy clouds drifted in the blue sky like sailboats. It was a perfect day in every way. She didn't want to ruin it by messy conversation, but she had to.

"Carter!'

"Yah."

"Carter, are you a lady's man?" she asked cautiously.

"What!! What do you mean by that?" he snapped.

Molly stared into his eyes trying to get a reading and said, "Carter, I saw you at the game when three girls waved you down on the field like they were trying to catch a bus."

Carter didn't like being pressed for something totally innocent. "Molly, what are you getting at?"

"Just what I said, Carter. I don't want to be with someone who plays around."

Carter gently grabs Molly by the shoulders and faces her towards him. Her freckles had become more playful with the sun exposure against her now pink skin. Man, was she cute.

"Molly, I don't like to explain myself to others. But I like you, so I will." Molly waited holding her breath. "Those were three girls who went to Western. I knew them when they were in Kalamazoo. They were in town and surprised me at the game. I had no idea that they were even coming."

"Were they more than friends?"

"Molly, no! They were more like acquaintances; just people I knew when I was at WMU."

"Good!" she uttered. "So, you aren't a playboy?"

"Holy cow, Molly. No! I'm not. This is the first true date I've ever had, and you're turning it into a nightmare."

Her lips pouted. "I'm sorry, Carter. I just want someone who is sincere. Who is honest and good."

Carter hugged her and said, "I think you found him."

"Well, I'm not sure, Carter. I just don't know."

The Ferry slipped into the dock at the island. The blast of the ship's horn startled and alerted those waiting to depart. Molly and Carter walked the ramp to board the boat along with their companions of doubt, hope, and confusion.

~ 50 ~

DAD WANTS TO MEET YOU

Carter entered the Ignacio commissary for a quick snack before heading up to work on some last-minute studies. Molly was serving as usual wearing the same outfit required by the kitchen crew: hairnet and grey uniform.

She looked beautiful to Carter. What she wore didn't matter. She was Molly. That's all that mattered to him, but, hopefully, a Molly that cared for him.

"Hi Molly," Carter smiled. "That was fun at Georges Island." He was hoping for a positive response from Molly and braced himself internally.

"I thought so as well. At least until I messed it up," she said with a slight grimace. "I am sorry, Carter."

He breathed a sigh of relief. "We'll start over," Carter urged kindly.

"Yeah. Let's do that," Molly said as her brown eyes glistened. "So, what would you like, Carter?"

"I'll have a Molly to go."

"Oh, Carter. You are a smooth one," she grinned. "Now, what will you have? There are people waiting."

He pointed to a premade chicken salad sandwich and a bottled water. "Those will do. I want to take them up to my dorm room."

"You got it," smiled Molly as she handed Carter his request. "And Carter."

"Yes, Molly."

"My dad wants to meet you."

....

Molly met Carter at Ignacio Hall on the following Friday. She was driving a beat up, old Ford Ranger with an extended cab and a ladder rack: ladders and all. Various colors of paint splashed the sides of the truck.

Carter was waiting in front of the hall. Molly jumped out of the driver's seat and walked boldly up to him.

"Well, let's get to work, buddy," she smiled. She was in complete contrast to the truck which was a mess. She had on faded blue jeans, a light tanned top, and a smile the size of Tennessee.

Carter couldn't help it but to give her a hug. "So glad to see you, Molly."

"Same here, Carter. My dad is looking forward to seeing you." She pointed to the truck and said, "Hop in!"

They got into the truck. The interior was blotched with paint stains. The cab area was filled with cans, brushes, rollers, and all sorts of equipment used for whatever job.

"Quite a ride you've got here," grinned Carter.

Molly shot him a quick look, "It gets me from point A to point B, Carter. That's all that matters."

"I like it. It reminds me of our truck back home. It reflects productivity and hard work."

"Are you trying to get on my good side, Carter?" she said.

"No. I mean it. But I also want to get on your good side," he smiled.

As Molly drove, she gave a brief background of the South End.

"You will like Southie," Molly said with pride. "It has some very uppity up sections with beautiful brownstones and trees lining the streets and then there are some seedier areas where normal people can afford to live."

Carter swiveled his head around to take in all the city had to offer. "This is so diverse," he said.

"More diverse than you think, Carter." The South End has people from nearly every race and religion. There are Irish, Lebanese, Jewish, Greek, Black, Hispanic folks. You name it we've got it." She smiled at him. She was proud of her community and the multiplicity of the neighborhood.

"Why are there so many different folks here?" asked Carter.

"Good question. It began when many groups settled here and then became even more varied with the change of time. Talking about the change of time, all this land was once marshland. The Neck as it is called that we drove over here on Washington Street was the only solid ground. The rest of it was once tidal marshes which were filled in with dirt from a town called Needham several miles away.

Here's a fact for you Carter. The original site of the Tea Party is now land as a result of the all the fill that was put into the water. Bet you didn't know that?"

"Molly, I didn't know a lot of this stuff. Thanks for the information. If I just hang with you, I'll get smarter every day," he said.

"Oh, Carter. You are a charmer. Here we are." Molly pulls the truck into the back area of an old complex off of Pine Street. She points up to a balcony on the second floor. "That's where we live, Carter."

Molly and he slip out of the car. Carter looks up and sees two men waving down at them.

"Hi Daddy!"

"'i sweetheart. Glad to see you brooehght de troehck back in one piece. So, dat moehst be carter?"

"Yes. It is, daddy."

"Well, bring de bahy oehp 'ere."

The man beside Molly's dad yells down, "Is dat you's, Cawtaw? I cants believes it."

"Guido, what are you doing here?"

"I's heres to sees my partna's little girl's boyfriend. And yous da guy?"

Carter looks at Molly tenderly and says, "I hope so, Guido. I hope so."

~ 51 ~

GETTING TO KNOW YOU

Mr. O'Malley was a true Irishman gentleman. Guido, on the other, was a yacker. It was difficult for any of the other three to get a word in edgewise.

"So's, Cawtaw. Hows dids yous guys meet?"

"I met Molly at B.C. She was working at my dorm."

Guido grins and says to Molly, "Did yas give hims one of yas pearly whites smiles, sweethearts, and bats your eyelashes like dis?" He demonstrates with his caterpillar eyebrows. He looked ridiculous, but it was hilarious. Everyone burst out laughing.

"Oh, Uncle Guido. You're crazy," she chuckled.

Mr. O'Malley then says to Carter in his thick Iris accent, "Wooehld you like sahmethin to drenk, me bahy? 'Ow abooeht a beer, sahme wine ahr sahme iresh whiskey?"

Carter could hardly understand what he said but caught some of the message and was able to respond. "I don't drink, sir."

Guido jumps in, "What's wrongs wit yas. Yous don'ts drinks, Cawtaw. I dint's knows dat?"

"Nor did I," said Molly. "I like you even more, Carter."

"Thanks, Molly. I have my good traits," he smiled.

Molly and Carter looked at each other.

"Oh, gawd. Yous guys. Knock its offs wit dis lovey doveys stuff. I's gonna haves a beer."

Mr. O'Malley then speaks, "Wooehld you like sahme water ahr sahda?" Then he says, "ahh, Carter. you dahn't 'ave to call me ser. bahb ahr bahbby'll do joehst fine."

Carter turns to Molly with a quizzical look. She chuckles, "He said would you like to have a drink of water or soda and that you can call him Bob or Bobby."

"Oh! Yes, sir. I mean Bobby."

"Which will it be, Carter? Water or a soda?" asks Molly.

The rest of the conversation was similar: a linguistic gymnastics exercise with the only one struggling to understand; that being Carter. However, Carter found out a lot about Molly and her family. They were Irish Catholic which he didn't know much about. Her mother wasn't there because she held another job cleaning in the early evening. Mr. O'Malley was a hard worker, a kind man, loved his family, and wanted nothing but the best for his baby girl. He made that very clear without threatening Carter, but finessed his message with diplomacy, sincerity, and compassion. Carter liked him even more.

Guido was also a good guy. He worked hard with his painting business and his driving gig. Carter thought he was part of the mafia because of the way he dealt with Vinny and the bribe money. As it turns out, Guido was just a well known character in 'Little Italy' in the North End. Everybody knew him and liked him. He had done a lot of painting favors for his friends, and they respected his commitment to keeping quiet.

The front door opened and a sweet voice called, "Hi! Is 'e still 'ere?"

"Yes, he is Momma."

"Well, hold on to dat lad. I want to meet him." She took a few steps toward Carter. "My, yooehr a good lookin' lad." She turns to Molly, "Ain't 'e, sweetie?"

"Oh, Momma. Don't give him a big head.

Carter extended his hand,"Nice to meet you, Mrs. O'Malley."

She gently batted his hand aside and gave him a gentle hug. "A little cozy fhr you, my lad. Mahlly has never brought a boy home. You must be special."

"Thank you, mam."

"It's Erin, lad. You can call me Erin."

The group spent a little more time together exchanging pleasantries. Carter had done well. They all liked him. He was humble, courteous, and likeable . . . as he always is. He was just being Carter.

Before they left, Mr. O'Malley had a question for his beloved daughter. He says, "Mahlly, if you wooehld like a few days at de cape, one o' me coehstahmers 'as a free rental available. 'e wants to repay a favahr to me."

"Oh, Daddy! That would be wonderful. Thank you! Thank you! Thank you!" She gives him a big hug and turns to Carter. "He likes you. He likes you a lot."

~ 52 ~

CAPE COD

The ride down to the Cape was enjoyable. Both Carter and Molly were looking forward to a moment of time where they could just relax and soak in the beach, the sun, and the sand.

When they got to West Dennis, they drove toward the Light House Inn and then took a left onto a sandy road called Uncle Stephens.

"Where are we going?" Carter asked.

Molly smiled excitedly, "You'll see." She drove a short distance to a little cul-de-sac which had cute cottages arranged around it and a big house facing the ocean. "That's the Beach House Inn," she said pointing to the big bed and breakfast inn.

"Is that where we're staying?"

"No! But my father did some work for the family who owns it, and they were able to arrange for us to stay at a little one-bedroom cottage on the beach about four houses back. I was hoping to see someone outside to thank them."

"That was nice of them."

Molly completed the drive around a little park which had a wooden pirate ship and swings in the middle and then headed for their cottage.

They drove into the sandy parking area behind a cute cottage and grabbed their belongings. A short trek through the sand got them to the back door. When they walked in, both of them gasped with astonishment. The house was small; very small. However, the location was perfect; right on the water with a beach and a stone jetty that extended out into the ocean. It was beautiful.

The accommodations were tight but quaint. The first thing they noticed, after being astonished by the view, was a fishing net hanging from the ceiling trapping a variety of sea shells. A sofa embraced the side wall with two chairs settled on each end. A little coffee table was in front of the seating area with Cape Cod magazines and flyers promoting local restaurants and stores. On the opposite side, stood a refrigerator and a stove.

Carter said, "This is cozy." He looked out the picture window at the ocean. "And a beautiful view. I can't believe this, Molly."

"It is pretty cool," she grinned.

The other part of the cottage was even smaller. It had a separate bathroom and a little bedroom with a double bed.

Carter walked into the bedroom and dropped his duffle bag on the bed. Molly was right behind him. "Not so fast, Carter. This is where I'm sleeping."

He gave her a puzzled look. "Where am I going to sleep?"

She backed up and pointed to the small sofa in the small living room with the small coffee table. "Right there, my friend."

That night they took a stroll down the beach. It was a clear evening, and the stars glistened in the sky. The waves lapped the shore and retreated back into the ocean. The motion repeated itself accompanied by the soft splashing, pulling sound of the water. It was like a serenade to them both.

They talked about school, their ambitions after graduation, and her families and friends. Carter shared with Molly stories of his best friend, Charli.

"Charli is the best. We ride horses together, chase pigs, go fishing, and even get in trouble once in a while." Carter looked out at the ocean as he talked. It was obvious to Molly that his mind had wandered off to Paw Paw and to his friend, Charli.

"Charli is *really a good friend*, Carter?" she asked him.

"Charli is the best friend I could ever have," responded Carter still staring out beyond the ocean. Hopefully, you'll meet Charli one day.

"Well, I hope it is someday soon. I want to meet this mystery person," Molly smiled.

~ 53 ~

HERE KITTY, KITTY, KITTY

In the morning, Carter decides to take a jog. It was warmer than he expected, and the sun didn't disappoint the few early bird sunbathers who rested on the beach. He rolls out of the sofa, gets dressed, and slips out of the cottage quietly, ensuring he doesn't wake up Molly in the bedroom.

He loved the quiet of the morning, with the only sounds being the croon of a few seagulls and the waves lapping the shore.

Carter was getting in a rhythm with his jog. As he ran, he soaked in the sites of the boats, the cottages, the ocean and more.

A person sunning herself down on the sandy beach caught his eye. And why not? She was stunning, tanned, well-exposed, and very well endowed. She wore a skimpy bikini which revealed her assets. A delicate gold chain hung around her neck, and two chains rested playfully surrounded her waist.

A massive bull of a man in black pants and a white collared shirt stood a short distance from her. He had on sunglasses and a thick gold necklace. His head seemed like a swivel as his eyes scanned up and down the beach.

Carter, being Carter, smiled at the woman and said, "Good morning. How are you doing?" as he jogged by and waved to the man.

She flashed a big smile and said, "Bettah now, sweetie."

The bull watched the verbal exchange intently and then surveyed the surroundings.

Carter kept on running and thought to himself, *WOW*. That said it all.

When he reached the end of the beach cut off by the Swan River, he sat on the rocks and reflected. His journey to Boston was coming to a close. He had met some incredible people and grew as a person. But he missed the simplicity of home, the cornfields, the horses, his family.

He forgot where he was until he felt the tender touch of fingers on his shoulder. He thought it was Molly. However, when he turned around, it was not Molly. Instead, it was the girl on the beach.

"Hi, I nevah got yah name," she smiled coyly.

Nervously, Carter replied, "Oh, my name is Carter."

"Cawtah. I like that. My name is Kitty."

"Well, it's nice to meet you, Kitty. But, ah, I better return to the cottage."

"I can walk pawrt way back with ya?"

"Well, I should really..."

Without letting him finish his sentence, she grabbed his arm and pulled him close. "Ah, come on, Cawtah," she said flirtatiously. "We can get to know each othah bettah."

As they were walking back to her towel, Carter kept resisting.

"I really have to get back, Kitty."

"Oh, Cawtah. Stop being such a baby. Tell me about yahself. Are ya working? Are ya a student? Do ya work out?" She squeezed his bicep. "Oohh."

"I play. . . ah, football," he sputtered.

"For tha Patriots?" she swooned. She pulled him in more closely. She was getting much too comfortable.

"No, I played for B.C, but I'm done now," Carter spurted. "I've got to go. Nice meeting you, Kitty."

Carter pulled his arm away from her grip and began jogging down the beach. "Nice meeting ya, too, Cawtah," Kitty grinned provocatively.

She watched him fade into the distance as he ran down the beach. She wasn't the only one watching. Aside from the bull, another man dressed in a multi-colored Hawaiian shirt and loud bathing trunks with fish plastered all over them stared at Carter as he disappear. His face was tight and gnarled. He was not happy.

~ 54 ~

KNOCK AT THE DOOR

Later in the day, Molly and Carter decided on their evening dinner plans. They debated between going to Paradise Pizza in Dennis or for a fish plate at Seafood Sam's in South Yarmouth. Seafood Sam's got the nod.

They began to gather themselves for their dinner when a hard rapping shook the screen door. "Who's that?" Molly asks Carter.

"I have no idea, but I'll soon find out," he grins as he heads to see who is knocking. Staring at him through the screen with the sun behind the visitor, stood a sturdy, muscular guy with a deep tan. He was wearing a colorful Hawaiian shirt and fish-spattered bathing trunks.

Innocently, Carter grins and says, "Aloha. Can I help you?"

"Oh, a funny guy. Yeah, you can help me," the man growls.

"I'll be glad to," Carter opens the door to let the man in. The guy takes one step into the cottage and unleashes a stiff fist, landing on Carter's face. Carter falls to the wooden floor like a bag of cement.

Molly rushes out of the kitchen and sees Carter crumpled on the floor, blood dripping out of his nose. "Carter, are you OK?" She screams.

The man leans over Carter's body and peers into his face. He snarls with spit coming out of his mouth,

"Stay away from my girl." He stands up, glances at Molly, and walks out slamming the door behind him.

Molly dashes for the door and yells out, "You better run, you creep." Then she turns abruptly to Carter. "What's going on, Lover Boy."

"I've never heard you shout before?"

"I have my moments. Don't change the subject. Are you messing around with someone in the morning on your *walks*?"

"No, Molly, I swear. I . . . "

"Oh, Carter. Shut up! I know you're not. You're too good of a man. Now tell me what happened to make that Bozo so mad."

Carter explained everything in detail, down from the skimpy bikini to the gold chains around her waist and neck.

"So, Carter. You want me to get a skimpy bikini?"

"Of course not."

"Well, you can at least buy me some gold jewelry. By the way, you wouldn't get me in one of those threads of cloth posing as a bathing suit for a million bucks. Like me for me. Not for," Molly was searching for words, ". . . for walking around half naked."

"It was a whole lot more than half naked, Molly."

"Oh, give it a rest, Carter. Sometimes I think you've gotten hit in the head too many times playing football."

~ 55 ~

AT LEAST CARTER'S PERSISTENT

The next morning, Carter wakes up at his usual time and puts on his shorts. Molly, half asleep, hears him in the living room and calls out, "What are you doing?"

Carter responds casually, "I'm going for my jog."

Molly wrestles herself onto her elbows, "What are you, crazy?"

"Molly, I didn't do anything wrong. I'm not going to let that guy dictate what I do. If I don't run, he wins."

"Oh, Carter. What is it with you football types all about winning?"

"It's not about winning. It's about standing up for what is right."

"Well, if you get punched in the snoot again, don't come running back to me for a band-aid." She then flops down in the bed and adjusts her pillow. "Hey, Carter."

"Yes!"

"Be careful."

Carter throws Molly a kiss and skips down the steps.

....

It's a beautiful Cape Cod morning, with the sun glistening off the gentle sea. Carter feels good, aside from the slight throbbing in his nose. As he gets closer to the beach where the bikini girl usually is, he sees the big guy with an open white shirt and gold necklace.

Then he sees Kitty walking toward the beach from their cottage with her towel. When she sees Carter, she starts running toward him. She throws down a towel in her spot and drapes her arms around him. "Are you OK, baby? Vito said he took care of you."

"I'm fine. I just want to continue my jog." He unwraps her arms and heads up the beach.

He gets to the Swan River and sits on one of the rocks on the jetty. He takes time to look out at the ocean and take in the views. Fishing boats were churning through the water, and a few sailboats glided effortlessly along the calm sea. The seagulls were squawking in flight. Some were chasing the boats hoping for an easy meal.

It was special. But Carter had to get back to the cottage and, more importantly, to Molly.

On his return trek down the beach, Carter sees Kitty and Vito. They are engaged in a heated, yelling match. The big guy is watching over verbal feud while occasionally looking up and down the beach. All three spot Carter.

"You, Jerk!" blasts Vito as he charges toward Carter. Carter steps to the side, and Vito lands face-first into the sand and pebbles.'

"Are you OK?" Carter says sincerely and extends his hand to help the guy up.

Vito slaps his hand away. "Yeah, I'm all right, loser. But yous won't be when I's finish with yous." He scrambles to his feet. The bull steps forward eager to help. His face distorted with toughness. Vito waves him off. "Oh, no, T. This loser is all mine."

Kitty is screaming, "Please, Vito. Just stop it. He din't do nothin'."

Vito makes another charge at Carter and misses but doesn't fall this time. He turns. He rushes Carter one more time, but he is off his mark again as Carter knows how to avoid tackles. He lands on his belly and slides headfirst into a boulder this time. He gashes his head and is dazed.

Kitty, the bull, and Carter rush to Vito's aid. Blood is dripping down his face, and he is groaning.

Suddenly, A shadow looms over from behind them. They turn to see who it is. "What's happening here?" Molly says calmly. She sees the blood oozing down Vito's face. "Do you have some gauze, hydrogen peroxide, and bacitracin?"

"Baci what?" asks Kitty.

Big T responds, "Yeah, we got some of dat stuff. All dat stuff."

"Well, go gets it," whines Kitty. "Can't yas sees dat Vito is hurt?" Molly looks at Carter and rolls her eyes.

Molly gets Vito all patched up and says, "You should go to the hospital and get some stitches."

"I ain't goin' nowheres. No one is goin' to knows I's here."

"We know you're here," said Carter with a foolish grin.

Suddenly, Molly slaps Shucks on the side of the head. She looks at Vito. "Well, have someone check out that gouge. It's pretty deep and severe."

"Yeah, yeah!" Vito blurts.

Molly stands and pulls Carter up. "We better go now." And they start walking back to their cottage.

"Thanks for your help, Sweetheart," shouts Kitty.

"Oh! No problem!" replies Molly.

"Not you, honey," Kitty smiles and sways her shoulders. "I'm talking to Cawtah. *That* sweetheart."

Molly abruptly grabs Carter's arm, "Let's go, you, dumbass," as she practically drags him down the beach.

Molly struts toward the cottage after letting go of Carter. He walks behind her and slows down, watching the steps in the sand multiply between them. Sirius clouds float high above. A seagull glides by and lands on an outstretched jetty.

Molly abruptly turns, "What are you waiting for, Carter?"

Cautiously, deliberately he says, "You called me a 'dumb A.'"

"Oh, Carter. What do you expect? I'm from Boston, grew up in the city, and am Irish."

"I just . . ."

"Just what, Carter? You grew up on a farm. You only had to worry about cows leaving the pasture or needing to tighten your horse's saddle," Molly's voice intensifies, " or pigs Or CHICKENS OR . . ."

Carter stared at her as her freckles became darker and her cheeks reddened. Her red hair glistened in the sun. Finally, he smiled, "You're right," he pauses slightly, "I'm sorry."

"What does that mean, Carter?"

"You're right. I'm not like you. I've got a lot to learn."

"How come you can't get mad? Why don't you let it go? You're always so . . ." Molly cut off her sentence, turned, and started walking away from Carter.

Throwing words at her back, "Molly, if I get mad. I lose control of my thoughts and my feelings." She keeps walking, and he follows her like a puppy. "I want to do what is right." Molly swings around and stomps up to him, glaring into his face, about to say something when Carter says, "You are so cute when you are mad."

"Carter, you make me so, so..," Molly stutters, trying to find the right word. Suddenly she puts her arms around Carter's neck, gently pulls him toward her, and kisses him softly.

"Does that mean you're not mad at me?" Carter blushes in surprise.

"No, Carter. That means that I'm the one who should be sorry, and that I love you. You're such a good man."

~ 56 ~

IGNATIO HALL VISITORS

Kathy sits in her Boston apartment overlooking the alleyway. Everything is expensive in Boston, so Kathy rented an affordable apartment. At least she was in Boston, so she could walk or take the trolley to wherever she needed to go. She was happy.

Her cell phone rings. She grabs it to check out the text message. It was from Joyce.
"Kathy, did you know that Carter is leaving for Michigan soon? You might want to say goodbye."
Kathy didn't have to wait for an invitation. She figured if she left now, she could catch a T and be at Ignacio Hall at around noon. This could be her last chance to make a pitch for the guy, her guy.
She brushed her hair back neatly and secured it with a clip. Next, she dabbed some makeup on her cheeks for color, applied light lipstick, and sprayed on her favorite perfume, Ralph Lauren's Romance. She then put on a semi-seductive pink blouse

and a short blue skirt. Finally, she checked herself out in the mirror and said, "Now, that should work."

....

Julie's plane landed at Logan at 11:00 a.m. Her meeting at Harvard didn't begin until 2:00 p.m. But, if she hustled, she could see Carter and congratulate him on getting his master's. This really is a big deal for Shucks, and she wanted him to know that.

....

Carter arranged to have his diploma sent home. He's not into pomp and circumstance and doesn't want to dress up in a gown and hat. Not that it wasn't appreciated. It was.

It was a big deal when he graduated from high school, especially considering his ADHD. He proudly stepped on the stage with his classmates to receive his diploma. He stood with his family for pictures. The whole nine yards.

When he graduated from Western Michigan, he was honored. But even then, the only reason he attended the graduation ceremony was out of respect for his parents. They basically lived in Kalamazoo, so proximity wasn't an issue. Another reason for participating was that he was graduating with a group of friends and players.

At B.C. Shucks hadn't developed the bonds in graduate school to make it a mutual event. His family would have to pay the expense of flying into Boston and staying overnight. He didn't want them to go through that. So, why go?

Charli knew Carter wasn't going to go to graduation and wanted to congratulate him at the school he was graduating from. So she told Carter that she was coming on this day: two days before he was to leave campus. However, she arrived earlier than he had expected.

The Uber driver dropped Charli at Ignacio Hall at around noon, just in time for lunch. She approached the courtesy desk as Carter was coming into the reception area to go to lunch.

"Is that you, Charli," he said in surprise.

"It sure is, Carter. I got here early. So, why wait?"

"Holy cow, Charli. You look beautiful." And she did. Her long dark hair was tossed playfully over one shoulder. She had casual makeup on, which accented her eyes. Her cheeks were rosy with a light application of whatever. Her smile lit up the room, and in a rare moment, she wore a black dress that clung to her slight body and came down to just above her knees. Her outfit was made complete with slightly elevated black Rita loafers. Charli was always a student of comfort.

"I don't think I've ever seen you in a dress," exclaimed Carter.

"Probably not, Carter, but this is a special occasion. So, I thought I'd dress up for you."

"Well, you sure clean up real good, Charli."

She smiled, "There you go, Carter. Always the master of the understatement."

They walked into the dining room. Carter peeked into the serving area to see if Molly was there. Mona and Cheryl were serving.

"Hi, Mona. Is Molly here?"

"She sure is, Carter. She's in the kitchen helping Kyle."

"And Kyle sure needs help," kidded Cheryl.

"Could you send her out to our table when she is available, Mona?"

"I sure will." As Carter walks away, Mono turns to Cheryl and says, "Do you see that girl Carter is with?"

"Yes, I do," says Cheryl. "Now that one, there is a real looker."

"I'll get Molly," Mona says gingerly. "This could be interesting.

~ 57 ~

MOLLY MEETS CHARLI . . . AND OTHERS

Molly walks out of the serving excited to see Carter. However, when she sees the beautiful girl, he is with, her jaw drops. "Well, Carter. Who do we have here," she says with a crooked smile.

Carter stands, as does the girl smiling from ear to ear. "Molly, this is my best friend, Charli."

Molly takes a huge gulp. Then, looking at Carter and pointing to Charli, she blurts, "That's Charli. I thought your best friend was a boy." She glances at Charli. Not a girl. A beautiful girl at that."

"Thank you," says Charli sweetly.

Molly looks annoyed and is annoyed. "I can't believe you brought 'your best friend' in to see me like this." She pulls off her hair net and waves it in his face. She looks at Charli. "She's all dressed up, and I look like a hag."

"You look great, Molly. You always . . ."

Mona and Cheryl are joined by Kyle at the serving booth to watch the show. The food line had stopped as well to see what was happening. Mona turns to her co-workers and says, "Oh, my. We may see Molly's Irish get crazy."

"Oh, Carter. Zip it. Sometimes I think you have bricks for brains," pouts Molly.

"Now, you and I think alike," remarks Charli. "Sometimes, this guy doesn't have a clue. But that is why he is my best friend. He never means any harm."

Molly absorbs Charli's statement. It was true. Carter was just a good person. A little dense at times, but, nonetheless, a good person.

Suddenly, a voice from the entrance to the dining area interrupts the trio,

"Carter. Thank goodness you're still here." Kathy runs up and throws her arms around him. "I heard you were leaving soon and had to say goodbye. Oh, Carter, I'm going to miss you so much.

Cheryl looks at Mona and Kyle, "Holy Moly. This is getting good." They all nod their heads in agreement while keeping their eyes on the action.

"Hi, Kathy," says Charli.

"Who are you?"

"Kathy, I was with Carter when he brought you..."

Carter jumps in, "You know, Kathy when you got drunk at the bar. Charli and I helped you out."

Molly and the entire dining population stared with amazement, thinking, is this guy really saying this stuff?

Kathy is mad. "I can't believe you just said that, Carter. I came all this way here to wish you well, and you make an announcement like that. I should..."

An attractive, professional woman walks up to the group and addresses Carter. "Hi, Carter. Just want to congratulate you on getting your degree." She looks at all the women. "Looks like you have quite an entourage.

Cheryl turns to Mona in the serving area and says, "This looks like an episode of *The Bachelor*."

"You got that right, girl," Mona replies. "We've got to rescue Molly." Then, she yells out, "Molly! Molly, girl! You've got to get back to work. We've got people waiting."

Molly looks at Charli, "It was nice meeting you, Charli, crazy as it is now. Maybe we can get together and chat, and I can find out more about *bricks for brains* as she stares at Carter. She turns and heads back to her work area.

Carter then says, "We'll see you later, Molly, when you're dressed up."

Kathy, Julie, and Charli look at Carter and say, "You really do have bricks for brains."

Carter thanks Kathy for coming and apologizes for being such a goof. Kathy accepts his apology but, in a weird way, is kinda glad that he tripped over his words. She didn't feel the emotional attachment that she did before. She liked him. Yes. But Shucks was not that guy. She gave him a hug and left.

Julie said flatly, "You'll never change, Carter. Thank goodness. Your innocence is a blessing even though you trip over yourself half of the time."

"Thanks, Julie. I think?" he replies.

"We'll keep in touch, Carter." Julie hugs him, starts to walk away, and gives him a wave over her shoulder. "I love you, Carter."

"I love you, too," he whispers.

Charli looks at Carter in amazement. "You are something else, Carter."

"It looks like it's just you and me, Charli," he grins.

"Not exactly," she says and points to the kitchen area where Mona, Cheryl, Kyle, and Molly are gazing at them. Molly's dark red hair is peeking out from her hairnet. Her freckles seem to vibrate on her cheeks, and her smile is lighting up the room.

"I guess it isn't exactly you and me, Charli," Carter murmurs. Gesturing toward Molly, "Do you like her, Carter?"

"No, Charli. I don't."

"Carter, you're crazy. She's beautiful and a hard worker. She's got spunk. She's . . .

"Charli. Charli, calm down. I don't like her." He pauses and looks in Molly's direction. She's smiling at him. "I love her."

"That's nice, Carter. But do you . . ."

"Do I what, Charli?"

Tears formed in her eyes. "But do you love me?"

Carter reached across the table and cupped her hands in his, "I'll always love you, Charli. You're my very best friend."

~ 58 ~

TYING THE KNOT

Carter did love Charli. He loved Charli like a sister, and Charli loved Carter like a brother. Their bond, their history, and their love for each other were unbreakable. But it was Molly who won his heart.

The wedding took place in the South End at the Holy Cross Cathedral. Charli was the maid of honor, and Emily, Carter's sister, was a bridesmaid, along with a few of Molly's cousins and best friends, Mona and Cheryl.

The Rex family sat near the front of the alter to celebrate their friends' son's wedding and their daughter's role as maid of honor. They had often thought that it would be Charli who walked down the aisle to marry Carter. But it was not meant to be.

Julie sat in the church as well to celebrate Carter's and Molly's marriage. She was happy for both of them. To her, it was the most important decision one makes: choosing your mate for the rest of one's life.

The ushers included Damon, Carter's brother, Jerry Collins, the linebacker from WMU, Hal Krause, Carter's roommate, and

Chris Greer, Carter's tutor at B.C., as well as Guido. Guido had to have a role in the wedding. After all, he was Bobby's pawtna. They dressed casually. So instead of wearing tuxes, they all had on blue sports jackets and tan slacks and striped green and orange ties, the Irish colors.

Carter's mother walked down the aisle, escorted by Damon. They were a cute couple. Mrs. Dixon had on a tan dress with ruffled sleeves.

Molly's mother was escorted by Guido to her seat on the left side of the first row. The priest, Father Adorno, then entered, followed by Carter and his father. Carter had insisted that his father be the best man since he had been the best man in his life. Mr. Dixon did not wear his overalls. He wanted to, and Carter didn't care if he had, but out of respect for the O'Malley family, Rachel insisted he wear a blue suit, as did Carter.

The bridesmaids were all beautiful, with simple green dresses and an orange sash draped over their left shoulders. One would think that would look odd, but it worked nicely. They were accompanied by the groomsmen.

The maid of honor then walked down the aisle alone. Charli looked like she could have been in a movie. She was gorgeous, with her hair pulled up and a few strands dancing down her cheeks.

She was followed by a young girl and boy, children of the O'Malley's cousins, who carried the rings and flowers. Both were cute and nervous.

When Mendelssohn's "Wedding March" engulfed the church. The small crowd turned around to look at the bride and her father. Mr. O'Malley's cheeks were rosy, and he had a grin from ear to ear. A slight tear trickled down his face and dropped to his sleeve.

Molly was the perfect bride. In contrast to her simple but elegant white gown, her auburn red hair accented the beauty she possessed. Her freckles seemed to frolic on her face, and her smile outshined any of the candles in the church.

Carter's heart nearly dropped. He was marrying an angel, and he knew it.

Seated quietly by themselves in the back of the church was a couple who just didn't seem to belong. Her dress was much too revealing, especially for the church. And the man was dressed just too casually for a wedding: white shirt opened and gaudy gold necklaces hanging from his neck like Mr. T.

"Wha da heck we's doin', here?"

"Oh, put a sock in it, Vito. I's jus wants to sees Cawtah ones last time."

~ 59 ~

EPILOGUE

Two Years Later

It was a beautiful spring morning in Holliston. The sun bathed the backyard with warmth, and its rays sliced through the window blinds creating a parallel pattern of light on the wooden kitchen floor. Carter sat at the table near the window with the same pattern of light resting on his face, his clothing.

He gazed out at the backyard and sighed. Their dog, Misty, lay on the warm, cement patio, oblivious to a rabbit hopping along the brook, stopping to munch on some greenery. A red cardinal fluttered down to the birdfeeder and helped himself to some seed. The tranquility of this moment reminded him of home. He loved nature, animals, and, especially, family.

He heard his wife giggling and urging the boys to get ready for their naps in the kids' bedroom. They began chuckling as she gently tickled them with her fingertips. Then a muffled quiet caressed the bedroom as the boys settled down. Finally, she switched on the white noise machine, and tranquility subdued the little guys.

Carter smiled to himself. He got a kick out of those rascals. The boys were full of energy, mischief, and curiosity. And, like their father, they smiled at everything and everybody.

But most of all, he loved his wife: her kindness, gratefulness, and goodness. Molly was everything a man could ask for and more.

She shuffled quietly into the kitchen, ensuring she didn't wake the twins up. She looked at Carter with tenderness and gazed up at his wife, his beautiful, patient wife. Her auburn hair glistened in the light streaming in through the window.

He smiled and touched her hand as she sat down at the kitchen table and said, "It's been a journey, Honey. But look where we are."

She smiled back at Carter and laid her hand on his. "It has been a journey." Then, she paused delicately, ". . . and you ended up with me."

"It was always you." He sighed, and gazed out the window, ". . . *It was always you.*"

Carter and Molly immersed themselves into the Holliston community. They both helped out at the food bank, went to Saint Mary's Church, Carter joined the Lion's Club and became a member of the Holliston Volunteer Fire Department. The couple felt strongly about helping others and did.

Carter volunteered as an assistant coach for the high school team. He also worked for the Kiley Insurance Agency, whose office housed in a refurbished barn tucked behind a historic downtown home. Gerry and Mary Kiley ran the agency, and one of their sons was the Holliston football coach, Todd Kiley.

Carter still fished. He and his buddy Hal would go to Lake Winthrop in Holliston, and Molly would accompany them at times with the twins Emmitt and Bobby wearing their little overalls.

But Carter's heart was still in Paw Paw, the farm, and his family. Molly, the twins, and he would travel as often as possible back to Michigan. Molly became close friends with Charli. They were like sisters. Charli taught Molly how to ride, and they usually rode off together leaving Carter back at the barn with the twins. Carter was a little envious. It was like he lost a little of his best friend, Charli, to, ironically, his wife.

But in his heart, he knew that he had made the right decision, the most important decision of his life: he married Molly. *It was always Molly.*

> "You can give without loving,
> but you can never love without giving."
> Robert Louis Stevenson

About the Author

Peter Alderman received an undergraduate degree from Western Michigan University and a Masters's from Boston College. He went on to be an award-winning educator. After teaching for thirty-seven years in Natick, Massachusetts, an annual scholarship was established in his name and John McKenna's name, a former principal, for their impact on students. They both were inducted into the education Wall of Fame at Natick High School. In addition, he has written several children's books: *Soccer Counts*, which he co-wrote with prolific children's author Barbara McGrath, and *The ABCs of Health*, a fun, colorful book that serves as an introduction to healthy foods for children.

The Rockets' Red Glare, a historical account of the origin of our national anthem, is accompanied by a CD by Platinum Award-winning artist JoDee Messina, was featured at the two-hundredth anniversary of the National Anthem, and is a popular educational resource.

Train Tracks was his first novel and is certainly not a children's book as it explores the darker side of life in a quick-moving, riveting style. It has received acclaim from readers all over the world.

The Good Man is the complete opposite of *Train Tracks*. It is a playful, heartwarming story of a young boy growing into manhood: a fun, moving read full of subtle drama, mystery, and football. Through mistakes, misjudgments, and lessons learned, the young man is guided in the right direction with the help of his parents, coaches, tutors, and female friends.

Peter now lives in Franklin, TN with his wife, Pam and their dog, Izzy. They gravitated to Tennessee when their sons moved to Nashville for job related reasons. They now have seven grandsons which keep them very busy and happy.

Peter with his high school sweetheart and wife, Pam.

ACKNOWLEDGEMENTS

Behind every aspect of one's life and accomplishments, there are people who guide, support and serve as pillars of strength. I would like to express my sincerest gratitude to the people who provided that foundation for me.

The most important person is my wife, Pam. She has been my angel and guiding light throughout my life. Everything I have ever been able to achieve or obstacles I have been able to overcome are because of her goodness, patience, and love. As I always tell her, "God sent me an angel."

To JoDee Messina whose life and music touched our family in more ways than she'll ever know.
To Francis Twarog, M.D, my cousin who earned a spot in my novel for being a role model to everyone.
To Michael Nierenberg, M.D. and his wife, Karen, who have given us cherished memories which last a life time.
To inspirational educators who earned character spots in my novel: Mimi Mclain, Fleur Mehal, John Buckley, and Ellen Maillet.
To Vinny Adorno, a retired firefighter and high school friend and his wife, Sue and to Robert O'Malley. To say they are good people doesn't say enough.

To Ed Mantenuto: a great administrator, hockey coach, and man.

To John Patrinari, store owner of Fiskes and a fixture to the Hollison community.

To Adrian Collins, the humble owner of Outpost Farm.

To the Sweeney, Grier, Krause, Woltors, Kiley, Rex, Morgan, Shanahan, LaRosee families for all they do for others.

To Louis McGrath, Emily Raffile, Julie McConchie, Scott McConchie, Allison Currie, Dave Randlett, Ross Randlett: our nieces and nephews who have navigated their lives to adulthood with amazing integrity and strength.

To Kathy Nolan, Joyce Cassidy, and Robyn Hutchins, our dear friends from high school.

To the Twarog, Pacosa, Alderman, and Fair families who were the glue to our families.

To our incredible neighbors and friends from Holliston. We miss you all every day.

To Paw Paw Athletic director, Alan Farnquist and head football coach, Dennis Stray, for their help in formulating information on the beautiful village of Paw Paw.

To Western Michigan University and Boston College for providing me and so many others with direction, skills, and motivation to navigate life's rough waters.

In memory of Mike Raftus who epitomized everything good.

There have been many people in our lives who reflect goodness. These are but a few folks who have elevated our lives.

Neal and Janet Ganley, John McConchie, The Donnellys, Father Flynn, The Scharff family, The Samuel family, Barbara McGrath, The Krauss Family, Dan Powell, M.D., Fernando Martinez, Tim Garber, Ken and Melissa Lewis, Monroe and Kathy Monroe, Rene Ciarametraro and Family, Roy and Maya Neeley, M.D. Omar Flores, MD, and, Serena Ezzeddine, M.D, Kathryn and Bill Julian, Susan Melanson, Kyle Fitts, Jim Yaggi, Jerry Collins, Rada Aponte, Mark Nemeskal, Corey Ring, Kareem Wright, Larry Lueth, Charlie and Joan Baugmann, Jessica and Brian Long, the Budwey family, M.D. and family, the Grier family, the Hendrick family, the Sweeney family. Danielle and James Drumwright, Dawn and Shaun Stauffer, M.D., Chuck and Katrina Tucker, Mona Gant, Cheryl Steele, Robert Kranc, Rick and Hope Rex, The Morgan &York families.

And my greatest appreciation to all the Natick educators with whom I had the good fortune to work.

Bob Macone, David Walker, John and Pat Rowan, Don Burnham, Kirsten McDonough, Ellen Maillet, Pam Robidoux, Ken Henderson, Maryann McGinty, Elaine Polansky, Andrea Taylor, Mimi McClain, Fleur Mehal, Ken Doyle, Amy Hawrylchak, Heather Moretz, Kerri Poissant, Ray Donohoe, Peter Souza, Barbara Doherty, John Buckley, Debbie Bresnick, Shannon Smythe Baird, Danielle Linkas, Nan Fleming, Louise Mikaelian, Kathy Kattany, Martha Curran, Judy Bickleman, Jim VonEuw, Kirstin Sokol, Harriet Safran, Ruth Evans, Ruth Nolin, Sarah Lane, Dennis Driscoll, John Hughes and so many others.

"A good man makes others good." – Menander

BOOK CLUB/EDUCATOR QUESTIONS

1. What was your favorite part of the book?
2. Which scene stuck with you the most and why?
3. What were obstacles that Carter had to overcome?
4. Which people in Carter's life had the greatest influence?
5. What was the most pivotal moment in Carter's life?
6. How do you feel about Emmitt and Rachel?
7. What are your thoughts about Charli?
8. How did the settings impact the story?
9. Which football feat spotlighted Carter's character?
10. Were there any characters with whom you could identify?
11. What endeared you to Guido if anything?
12. What were Carter's most admirable qualities?
13. How did coaches help Carter's maturation?
14. What was the most interesting historical fact you learned?
15. If you could trade places with any character, which one would it be and why?
16. What virtues did Molly possess?
17. How would you compare Molly and Charli?
18. What strengths did Julie have and how did she influence Carter?
19. What lessons were examined in The Good Man?
20. Who did you think or hoped Carter would marry?

Praise for *Train Tracks*

Peter Alderman has given us a precious and unforgettable gift with TRAIN TRACKS. Buckle up, and enjoy the ride!
—**Howard A. Klausner**
Screenwriter, Director, and Producer of such films as "Space Cowboys" starring Clint Eastwood, "The Identical" with Golden Globe nominated Ray Liotta, "The Last Ride", "The Secret Handshake" and "The Grace Card."

Alderman brilliantly tackles the trials and challenges inherent in the human condition.
H.T. Manogue, Award-Winning Author

What Readers Are Saying About *Train Tracks*
- free shipping at the Barnes & Noble websight

"Everyone needs to read this "think piece!" J. Cassidy

"*Train Tracks* is a compelling story. Bravo Peter Alderman!" R. Rex

"Amazing read!! The story pulls you in from page one, and it so hard to put down. Highly recommend!!!" Erica

"Peter's plot was shocking. Quite a story! Congrats for tackling such tough subjects!" Customer

"I can't stop thinking about it. Absolutely AMAZING!" Customer

"*Train Tracks* opens the reader's eyes to a world many of us have not experienced, but one we should all recognize exists." R. True

"Once started, *Train Tracks* is hard to put down. A true page turner." MJD

www.ingramcontent.com/pod-product-compliance
Lightning Source LLC
LaVergne TN
LVHW021811060526
838201LV00058B/3336